The Eyes of Pharaoh

Chris Eboch

Cover Art and Design by Lois Bradley

Interior Illustrations by Rollin Thomas

For everyone who has dreamed about ancient Egypt....

The Eyes of Pharaoh

Chapter 1

Waset, Egypt
Year Seven, Day Five of the First Month of Summer
in the reign of Pharaoh Ramses the Third

Seshta ran. Her feet pounded the hard-packed dirt street. She lengthened her stride and raised her face to Ra, the sun god. Her *ba,* the spirit of her soul, sang at the feel of her legs straining, her chest thumping, her breath racing.

She sped along the edge of the market, dodging shoppers. A noblewoman in a transparent white dress skipped out of the way and glared.

Seshta glimpsed women sitting cross-legged beside large baskets, peddling sandals, flat bread, or linen dresses. She heard voices raised in argument and in laughter. The smell of roasting lamb from a street stand brought saliva to her dry mouth.

Two soldiers stopped in mid-conversation to watch Seshta pass. One of them called out, "Hey, pretty girl, what's your hurry?"

Seshta grinned but didn't slow. Why walk when you could run?

She held up her linen dress and hurdled a pile of manure and garbage reeking in the sun. The sunlight grew brighter as she left the narrow market streets, and she caught a whiff of decaying reeds.

At the docks, Seshta turned onto a wide dirt path. She ran upstream, dodging sailors and travelers. Ships crowded the riverbank. Their square sails rose above wooden hulls painted blue, red, white, and green. Merchants shouted orders to the men loading or unloading their ships.

The bustle faded as she reached the edge of the city and ran between the riverbank and golden fields of grain. Seshta eased her pace, letting the voice of her heart slow.

She loped to the last pier, one large enough only for fishermen and their small craft. At the end, her friend Horus lay on his stomach, peering over the edge at the water. Seshta flopped down beside him. He glanced over, his black eyes smiling in a broad face tanned as dark as the river's mud. His shaved scalp gleamed brown in the sun.

Seshta took a deep breath and released it. The breeze dried the sheen of sweat on her skin. "Greetings, oh most talented of youths."

"A glorious day to you, graceful maiden of the great goddess Hathor."

Seshta grinned and gave up the mock formality. "What are you doing?"

Horus leaned over the water, pulled on a string, and hauled in a wooden boat as long as his hand. He passed it to Seshta and she studied the replica of the swift racing ships loved by rich nobles. The toy was unpainted but perfect in every detail, with a linen sail and delicate rigging. The center held an open cabin. The prow curved up into a carved ram's head. The boat needed only a miniature crew to bring it to life.

"It's wonderful!" Seshta said. "You'll sell that in no time."

"If Sunero thinks it's good enough, he'll finish it and put it in the shop."

"Hah! Sunero doesn't want to admit that you're already a better toymaker than he is. He's afraid he'll lose you as his apprentice—and the money your toys bring him."

Horus shrugged. "Sunero keeps my family fed."

"You've given him five years. You should have your own shop now."

"When is your contest?"

Seshta smiled and let him change the subject. Horus believed his place was determined by the gods, though she thought he deserved more from life. "Six days. The high priestess is working us harder than ever. I have this new acrobatic move I've only been practicing in private. Nothing short of a magic spell will keep me from winning that contest."

A shout came from behind them. "Greetings!"

Seshta sprang to her feet and waved to their friend Reya as he drifted toward them in a small skiff of bound papyrus reeds. He poled the skiff up to the dock and tossed the mooring rope to Seshta. She wrapped it around a post while Horus propped himself on one elbow to watch.

Seshta grinned as Reya vaulted onto the pier. Above his white kilt, the muscles of his chest and arms gleamed like bronze in the late-afternoon sun. He was three years older than Horus and Seshta, a man now at sixteen, and she always felt proud that he still chose to see his childhood friends.

Reya's teeth flashed white in his handsome face. He dropped a pair of brown and white geese at Horus's feet and said, "For your mother, with my compliments."

Horus picked up the dead birds. "Look how plump they are!"

Seshta said, "And you have nothing for a maiden of the temple of Hathor?"

Reya pulled her toward him and kissed her cheek. "Just my undying affection."

Seshta sniffed. "I don't know if I can persuade the goddess to accept such a cheap offering."

"Keep it for yourself, then."

"My mother will be delighted," Horus said. "And my sister. Your gifts are a blessing to them."

Reya shrugged. "It gives me an excuse to hunt." He pulled a sling from the waistband of his kilt and fitted a pebble into the woven pouch. He squinted at the next pier, some thirty paces away, swung the sling around his head by the straps, and let the pebble fly. It hit the post of the other pier with a *thunk* that carried across the water. Two sailors chatting on that pier jumped and looked around.

Seshta yawned and tried to look unimpressed.

Reya laughed. He turned to Horus. "Is your sister well?"

"Oh, yes. Webkhet is getting quite plump from your meat. She and Mother will miss you when your battalion goes to the field. Seshta and I will, too."

"Yes," Seshta said. "Life will be so dull without you to cause trouble. Do you know yet how much longer you'll be in town?"

Reya leaned toward them and whispered, "Maybe forever. Maybe I won't go back to the battlefields."

"Really?" Seshta tried to disguise her pleasure. "Didn't they want you once they heard you snore?"

He pinched her side and she yelped.

Reya waggled his eyebrows. "I have bigger plans. Stay by me, little girl, and you won't have to win that contest to meet royalty."

"Oh, no, what are you up to?"

He blinked wide, innocent brown eyes at her. "Who, me?"

Seshta shrugged and wandered off a few steps. "I don't suppose it's anything important. You're probably just bragging again."

In a singsong voice, Reya taunted, "I have a secret and Seshta doesn't know it."

She stamped her foot. "Oh! You donkey!"

Laughing, Reya grabbed her and twirled her around. "Sorry, my princess, but this I can't share, even with you."

"Why did you say anything if you didn't want to tell us?" Horus said. "Give her a hint or she'll go crazy."

Reya held Seshta at arm's length. "All right. One word, and that's it. If I give you this hint, you have to promise not to ask more. Strange forces are at work, and it could be dangerous for you to know too much. And you can't let anyone else know what we've said."

She sighed deeply and rolled her eyes. "Fine. What's your silly hint?"

Reya glanced around as if making sure no one else could hear him. "Libu."

"What?" Seshta snorted. "Who cares about those smelly heathens? They have nothing to do with us."

Reya's grip tightened on her arms. He stared into her eyes, his smile gone. "When you're at the center of the world, everyone cares about *you*, and that's enough."

Seshta squirmed out of his grasp. She rubbed her arms where he'd held her. "Egypt is the only country that matters. The Libu are Sand Dwellers, desert nomads, wandering cow-herders."

"They're warriors who see Egypt as a land where wine and oil flow freely. They want what we have."

"Look, I know you have to fight our enemies sometimes, but they could never win. Everyone knows Egypt is the most favored of all the lands and will reign in glory forever."

Reya shook his head. "Just because everyone knows it doesn't make it true."

Seshta sighed. "I have better secrets than that, and more important things to worry about than what's happening in strange foreign lands."

Reya smiled. "Yes, your big contest. All right, let's see what you can do. Give us a show."

Seshta took a few steps backward. She pulled off her linen dress and tossed it aside to dance bare, as all dancers did. She didn't have the long, braided wig that would brush the ground when she did a backbend. She wasn't wearing the strings of beads around her waist, wrists, and ankles that would rattle to the rhythm of the music. She didn't even have music to guide her, but Seshta raised her face to the sun and smiled.

She heard the music in her mind and began to sway. She tapped her feet on the pier, dancing intricate steps as light as the feather of truth. Her arms wove patterns through the air.

As the music in her mind swelled, she added leaps and spins. She did a backbend, and from there kicked her feet up into a handstand. She balanced, with her legs straight up, for three long breaths, then arched her back and bent her knees. Still balanced on her hands, she formed her body into a circle, until her toes brushed the back of her head. Then she bent her arms to lower herself until her chest touched the wooden pier. She rolled down to her knees.

The sun god seemed to pour his rays into her. Her *ba* soared like a bird.

Still kneeling, Seshta kept dancing, her hips swaying, back arching, arms caressing the air. Finally she leaned back, slowly, until her head rested on the ground. She stayed there, eyes closed, letting the joy of the dance wash over her.

Then the cheering started. Seshta's *ba* settled into her body like a tired pigeon coming home to a cozy roost. She opened her eyes, sat up, and smiled. Several people along shore had stopped to watch. Seshta gave a regal nod.

"Fantastic!" Horus said.

Reya shook his head. "Who would think such a little girl could dance like that?"

Seshta frowned and turned away to retrieve her dress. She was a better dancer because she was so slim. Many of the girls had to give up acrobatics when they grew heavy with women's curves. But she was not a little girl.

She pulled on her dress and turned to the boys with a smile to hide her irritation.

"You're really too good for the temple," Reya said. "It's a pity more people can't watch you."

Seshta's smile widened. Should she tell him her dream? She stepped toward him. "Do you know what I really want?"

Reya dragged her across the pier in a clumsy dance. "A handsome soldier for a husband?"

Seshta giggled. "Don't be silly."

"Come, my sweet, I will make you queen of all Egypt. Well, of Waset. All right, our neighborhood. At the very least, you shall be queen of my house. Or those parts of it not already claimed by my mother."

Seshta pushed him away. "You're impossible."

"No, just very, very difficult." He turned to gaze at the sun as it dropped toward the western horizon, standing as if posing for a royal statue. "I must go. I have dangerous work ahead. I should have seen the general the moment I discovered the situation, but I wanted to see you two first... just in case something goes wrong and I don't return."

Seshta and Horus looked at each other and shook their heads.

"Will you be here tomorrow?" Reya asked.

"I can be," Seshta said, "if the priestess is satisfied with our work early enough."

Reya kissed her cheek, patted Horus's smooth head, and stepped into his skiff. Horus leaned over to untie the mooring rope.

"Tomorrow, then," Reya said, "and I'll have news. Remember, not a word to anyone else."

His face clouded. He looked suddenly much older. "You'll see whether foreign lands matter or not." He grabbed the pole and pushed off. The skiff skimmed along the water while the river turned golden in the evening sun.

"You don't think he really knows something serious?" Seshta asked.

Horus hesitated. "Reya likes to show off. It's probably nothing important."

Seshta nodded. "I'd better head back to the temple. We're supposed to be resting."

Horus laughed. "You work harder at rest than most people do at their work."

Dancing never felt like work to Seshta. She longed for the freedom to do nothing but dance, to practice all day and perform all night.

She had to win the contest.

Seshta inhaled air tinged with rich mud and the sweet scent of lotus blossoms. It was cooler now, but the last rays of the sun still warmed her skin. A flock of geese honked overhead as they flew off to their evening roost. Singing drifted across the water from a fisherman in a distant skiff. He draped his net like a black spiderweb over the rosy glow of sunset on the river.

How could any place else matter, compared to this perfection?

Seshta smiled at Horus, turned, and ran for home.

Chapter 2

Seshta's *ba* soared in lazy circles, rising higher on warm air currents. Below, the Nile River spilled its banks, bringing fresh, rich mud to the farmlands. Green tendrils shot up, grew, and burst into heads of barley and emmer wheat. A faint humming might have been priests chanting their daily prayers or the cheerful song of farmworkers. All was as it should be, a land of peace and protection.

The Sun God's chariot dropped over the western horizon. The last glow of day turned the Nile's waters red.

The distant humming grew louder. A black cloud rolled down from the north. The noise shook the air so Seshta's wings trembled. The black cloud spread over the fields, a million locusts devouring every shred of grain.

The ground cracked apart like a mud bank in summer. The Nile waters turned to blood and poured into the cracks, racing in jagged lines across the fields.

A cry shattered the air. Seshta looked up at a dark form hurtling toward her. She screamed and beat her wings, trying to fling herself back and away.

A curved beak opened in a shriek as the enormous black bird barreled past her.

Seshta awoke trembling. She stared into a patch of blue, searching frantically for the monstrous bird. Then her mind cleared, and she realized the blue was just paint on her ceiling. She sat up in bed and pressed a hand to her chest.

What had the dream meant? With its curved beak, the bird had to be a falcon. Was it Horus, Lord of the

Sky, the falcon-god son of Osiris and Isis? Had he been threatening her or warning her?

Seshta leaped up to pace her small room. Had the dream been a message about her friend Horus? But Reya was the one involved in something dangerous. Had the falcon even been the god Horus, or one of the other falcon gods?

She rubbed her hands over her face. It was impossible to know without asking a priest to interpret the dream. She could do that. But not here, not in her own temple. She didn't want everyone talking about it.

She heard the call to prayer. She would have to wait until she could slip away, find some priests at another temple. She took a deep breath to still the voice of her heart and stepped out to meet the day.

Seshta's body did its part during the calisthenics exercises, the chants to the goddess, and the offering rituals. Her mind roamed on its own, circling from Reya's warning to her chilling dream. She had promised Reya she would tell no one about his vague hints. Did that mean she couldn't even ask a priest to interpret her dream? She wouldn't have to mention Reya.

But she couldn't take the chance. She couldn't risk betraying a promise to a friend.

She and Horus were on their own.

At lunchtime, she nibbled on bread and grapes without tasting them. Reya was a braggart, of course. He always had been, since they were young children. When he joined the army, he'd told endless stories about the brave deeds he would do. He planned to come home wealthy, famous, and beloved by all. Seshta and Horus teased him about it, and Reya would laugh, too. He loved life too much to get into real danger, though.

But that dream....

Jewelry tinkled as another girl knelt on the mat beside her. "Oh, Seshta!" Sit-Hathor's voice oozed sympathy. "You look tired. I hope the pressure of this contest isn't getting to you."

Seshta raised her eyebrows and studied Sit-Hathor, who wore a pleated dress of the finest linen, even here with no one to see her but the other dancers. Most of the girls, like Seshta, wore just a narrow scarf or string of beads tied around their waists.

"Thank you for your concern." Seshta looked back at her food.

She could feel Sit-Hathor frowning at her, but her rival's voice stayed honey-sweet. "I suppose you have something *marvelous* planned for the contest. We'd all love to see your routine!"

"You'll see it during the contest," Seshta said.

"Isn't that a bit of a risk? Don't you want feedback from your friends to make sure you don't embarrass yourself in front of Pharaoh?"

"I'll take my chances."

They held each other's gaze for a moment. Sit-Hathor gave a little "hrmph," rose gracefully, and flounced away. She sat next to her friend Idut and whispered rapidly, shooting scowls at Seshta.

Seshta plucked another grape. Reya had to be telling stories again. But she remembered the way he had looked into her eyes, and the grape hovered halfway to her mouth, forgotten.

Someone giggled behind Seshta. Little Miw leaned forward and whispered, "She's mad to know your routine. When you slipped out yesterday, she swore you were somewhere practicing secret moves. She's offered her faience lotus-blossom necklace to anyone who follows you and tells her what you do."

"Oh, please! I suppose now I'll be tripping over Idut every time I turn around." Idut was Sit-Hathor's best friend, if you could call it friendship. Sit-Hathor treated Idut more like a servant. Seshta wrinkled her nose. "Sit-Hathor should spend her time practicing, instead of worrying about me."

"Oh, she's practicing," Miw said. "That's why she can't follow you herself. She was at it for hours yesterday, long after the rest of us collapsed. Have you noticed her backbends lately?"

Seshta scowled. Sit-Hathor's backbends were the envy of the temple.

Sometimes being a temple dancer hardly seemed worth the trouble, with the tedious rituals and the other girls' petty gossip. But after the contest Pharaoh himself would know she was the best in the land. Then she could leave the temple and become a performer. She'd dance at parties, maybe even in the palace itself. Royalty would know her name and shower her with gifts. And all for doing what she loved most in the world.

If only Sit-Hathor's backbends weren't so good.

Finally the girls finished their duties, and the priestess swept away, leaving the scent of her jasmine perfume. At last Seshta could get back to the river with Horus and Reya. She'd find out what Reya meant. Probably he'd admit he was joking. Then she could forget about it and focus on the dance contest.

Some of the girls drifted toward their rooms or sat near the fountain to talk. Miw and Idut grabbed some leather balls and began juggling them back and forth. Seshta dashed to her room and pulled on her simple tunic, then slipped toward the main gates.

She paused between the tall pillars and glanced back. Half a dozen girls crept along the courtyard wall after her.

Seshta scowled. She practiced her new twisting handspring only at night, in the privacy of her room. But still, she didn't want an audience hanging around while she met Horus and Reya. She could leave the temple complex another way, over one of the walls, or out the back door where the kitchen got deliveries.

But that would waste time. She wanted to see Reya now.

The girls leaned against the wall, pretending to chat while they watched her.

Seshta smiled at them and waved. If they wanted to know where she went, they could just try to catch her. She ran.

By the time she reached the market, a few girls had already given up, and the others trailed far behind. The best athletes were focused on the contest; they wouldn't waste energy chasing someone for a necklace.

Seshta darted down one of the market alleyways. She jumped over a basket of dried catfish, earning a curse from the woman selling it. Seshta dodged around a fat man and nearly tripped over a naked child squatting in the dust. She turned a corner and stopped to catch her breath.

A lanky, bearded man stood arguing with a merchant. The merchant was clearly Egyptian, with his smooth face and shoulder-length wig. He wore a pleated kilt and a linen robe sewn with colorful embroidery. The other man's curly beard was enough to show he was foreign. He wore a cloak of black cowskin and no other clothing except a piece of leather fastened around his waist. His light brown hair had a thick braid on one side.

Could he be a Libu? He spoke Egyptian with a strong accent, complaining about the price of the merchant's arrows.

The Libu—if that's what he was—glanced at Seshta. She blushed and hurried away. She darted around a few more corners and then came out of the market several blocks from where she'd entered it. No temple girls in sight.

Seshta jogged toward the river. She would ask Reya if Libu men wore their hair in a side braid. She thought so, but maybe that was Hittites or Assyrians. Seshta's father had several Hittite slaves, but they were practically Egyptian now, after living here so long. Some had even been born in Egypt.

Seshta didn't have anything against foreigners. She couldn't blame them for wanting to come to Egypt, the best place in the world. But she couldn't believe the Libu mattered as much as Reya said. She scowled as she ran. She'd make him explain soon.

At last she reached the dock. Horus sat on the end of it, trailing a fishing line in the water.

Seshta trotted across the wooden boards. "Where's Reya?"

"I'm glad to see you, too. Reya's not here yet."

"Oh." Seshta flopped onto her back and stared at the sky. A hawk soared in lazy circles overhead. Seshta remembered her dream, and her *ba* fluttered in her chest. She rolled over and stared at the river.

Horus watched his fishing line, seeming content to sit there forever. Downstream, laundrymen sang as they worked at the river's edge. Two men washed clothes in large tubs, their shaved heads glistening and their loincloths drenched. Two others beat clothes clean on stones, and one spread the garments out to dry.

Seshta sighed. "What do you think of his story yesterday? His big secret?"

"Probably just showing off to impress you. But with Reya, you never know."

"Well, we'll find out when he gets here. He's not putting me off today!"

Horus glanced at her and smiled. "No."

"I wish he'd hurry." She slapped out a rhythm on the dock. "This is boring."

"He'll be here when he gets here. You can't change time."

Seshta sighed. Once she knew Reya was safe, she could curse him for distracting her and get back to more important matters. She needed to concentrate on dancing, not waste her time worrying about strange foreigners.

Ra, the sun god, carried his fiery burden toward the western horizon. Horus caught three catfish. A flock of ducks flew away quacking. Dusk settled over the river, dimming shapes and colors until they blurred to gray. The last fishing boats pulled in to the docks, and the fishermen headed home.

But Reya never came.

Chapter 3

Seshta gazed longingly at the morning sunlight streaming in through the doorway. Finally the priestess said, "All right, you may go. Enjoy your free day. Remember to *rest*."

The girls' chatter erupted like a pot boiling over.

"I can't wait to see my brother—his garrison is stationed here now."

"Cook always makes me the most wonderful meal when I'm home."

"Do I look all right? If my mother finds out I've been sick, she'll call the physician, and last time he put crocodile dung up my nose...."

Seshta pushed through the crowd. Today she would talk to Reya, no matter what. She couldn't bear any more waiting, or frightening dreams. She needed to focus on her dancing.

Miw walked beside her across the courtyard. "Are you going home today?"

"Yes." She would have to stop at home first, but then she'd hunt down Reya. "What about you?"

Miw shrugged. "My father won't be there. He's working on an investigation in Memphis." Miw's mother had died; her father was one of the Eyes and Ears of Pharaoh, a leader of the secret police.

"Oh? I suppose he's gone a lot."

Miw sighed and fiddled with the string of beads around her waist. "It's a position of great honor, of course, but I wish he were home more. He's always chasing some smuggler or investigating a plot against Pharaoh."

"I don't see my father much even when he's home." At least that would make it easier to leave and find Reya.

Miw grinned. "Well, at least I'll have plenty of time to spy on you today!"

Seshta's thoughts stumbled. Why would Miw be interested in Reya? Then she remembered Sit-Hathor's bribe to the girls. "Oh, Miw, not you, too?"

Miw shrugged. "It's something to do. Spying is fun."

Seshta tried to smile back as she edged away. "Have fun, then." She wondered what spy tricks Miw's father had taught her. Of course, Seshta had nothing to hide. Even if someone saw her new dance move, they wouldn't be able to copy it, not in the few days they had left before the contest. The other girls just weren't that good... except, perhaps, for Sit-Hathor.

She pushed the thought aside. Today, her focus was Reya. But she didn't want the girls following her while she looked for him. Until she understood his talk of secrets, she would keep his.

Miw, Idut, and two other girls trailed after Seshta as she left the temple. She strolled through the dusty streets, because she wanted the girls to see that she really was going home. Then she could slip out the back and lose them before she met Horus.

At her father's estate, Seshta stopped to talk to the young gatekeeper. "Nebra, some girls are following me. Don't let them in."

He squinted down the alley at the approaching dancers. "But aren't they friends of yours from the temple?"

"Yes, but I don't want to see them today. Don't let them in, no matter what they say. And don't leave your post!"

Nebra chuckled. "Is this some game you're playing? All right, I'll help."

"Thank you." Seshta trotted toward a small building within the walled enclosure. She found her father leaning over a table covered with papyrus scrolls and small clay tablets. One of his scribes sat cross-legged on the floor, scribbling a letter as Seshta's father dictated.

"—must receive the tri-annual account statement by the first day of the third month of summer. Please do not be late again, or the penalty will be deducted from your own pay."

"Father!"

"Oh, hello." He glanced back at the scribe. "Sign and seal that, and take it to the messenger."

"Yes, sir." The scribe scurried from the room.

Seshta's father sorted through a pile of scrolls, mumbling.

"Father?" She moved closer and touched the edge of his desk.

"Hmmm?" He spread out a scroll and scanned it, his lips moving.

"Father, can you tell me about the Libu?"

He blinked up at her. "The Libu? I do some business with them, though not as much as with Greece or Nubia."

"What are they like?"

"Demanding. Very forceful. They always think you're cheating them, and they'll try to get more from you at the last moment, more than you've agreed. They don't even seem to care that I'm representing Pharaoh, the Living God. They're suspicious of each other and even more suspicious of us. But they have good cattle and hides."

"Are they dangerous?"

"What? Oh, I imagine some of them would slit your throat if they thought you were cheating them. But surely you don't have to deal with Libu at the temple." He started to pick up another scroll.

Seshta leaned down to stay within his view. "I mean, are they dangerous to all of us—to Egypt. Are they trying to invade or anything like that?"

He squinted at her. "My dear, how could they? We have soldiers stationed at the frontier. And the Libu aren't very well organized. There are four major tribes in that region, and they fight one another more often than they work together." He looked down at the scroll and began mumbling, "Seven... forty-two.... No, no... one hundred and twenty-eight. Disgraceful."

Seshta straightened and inhaled, her nostrils filling with the sweet scent of the cedar chests that lined the walls. Reya must be wrong, then. But why hadn't he come to the river? And what did her dreams mean?

Her father looked up and stroked his chin. "Of course, they certainly might *try* to attack. They've done it before. The pharaohs Seti, Ramses the Second, and Merneptah all went to war against the Libu."

Seshta stepped back. "But... but that was a long time ago. And we always won."

Her father smiled. "Yes, I suppose it would seem a long time ago to you. And we did win, of course. I doubt any attackers today could get through the delta. We are fortunate to have a strong pharaoh in Ramses the Third." He cleared his throat. "Now I really must review these accounts. Run along and get something to eat."

He bent over his papyrus, head tucked between his hunched shoulders. Seshta stepped outside and stood blinking in the bright sunlight. She wasn't sure what she had learned, but at least she'd had more conversation than she usually got from her father.

She glanced toward the gate. Miw smiled up at Nebra. He was laughing while the other girls huddled together just beyond them. Idut pointed at Seshta and tried to sneak behind Nebra. He caught hold of her arm as she went by, and she squealed.

Miw darted toward the courtyard, but Nebra grabbed her around the waist and swung her back out the gate. Miw staggered into the other two girls. She straightened up, laughing and scolding Nebra, who was dodging Idut's kicks.

Seshta chuckled. Let them distract each other; she would get out another way. She walked along the tree-lined path to the family temple. She entered hesitantly, as always, afraid that her stepmother might have removed her mother's statue.

Her mother's carved wooden face smiled at her from its niche across the room. Seshta relaxed. The offering bowl in front of it overflowed with flowers, fruit, and bread. At least the servants were making sure Seshta's mother got food for the afterlife. Her tomb in the valley held everything she needed, both real goods and painted images, but Seshta liked to know her mother's spirit still had a home here, too, even if another woman slept in her bed.

Seshta sat cross-legged and looked up at the statue. "Good morning, Mother. I hope you are well. I guess you must be. I wish I had some good news for you. I told you about the contest—that's still the only thing the girls talk about at the temple. I was so excited, but now—you remember Reya? He's missing, and I'm worried. Will you look out for him? And give me guidance, so I can find him. Then I can get back to dancing. I'm going to win this contest and make you proud."

Seshta sighed. She felt so close to her mother here. If only her mother could reach across the barrier and speak to Seshta! At festivals, the statues of gods sometimes answered a question with a nod of the head. Even that would be enough.

Seshta closed her eyes, trying to reach into her own *ba*, to let it fly free the way it did when she slept.

She breathed deeply, letting the voice of her heart slow. Breath by breath, the world seemed to slip away until she felt like she was floating.

Seshta reached out with her *ba*. She seemed to feel another presence, faint as the fluttering of a moth's wings. "Mama?" Seshta whispered in her mind. "Is that you?"

Seshta heard no words, but a feeling of love wrapped around her.

Seshta wanted to keep floating in the loving embrace. But she needed help. "Mother, is Reya really in trouble?"

Seshta slowly opened her eyes. Her mother's statue seemed to glow. The face no longer looked painted, but real. Seshta blinked back tears as she gazed at her mother's smile.

The light trembled, and the statue nodded.

Seshta gasped. Her heart leaped wildly.

The air cleared, and once again Seshta sat solidly in the family temple.

Seshta's thoughts twisted and tumbled. She had done it! She had reached her mother's spirit! Her mother remembered and loved her. But an aching loss filled Seshta now. Why had she let her slip away so quickly? And she couldn't forget what her mother's nod had meant—Reya was in trouble.

Should she try to reach her mother again? But the way her heart raced and her thoughts jumped, she knew she would fail. She rose, kissed her mother's painted face, and went on to the house.

She passed through the entrance hall and reception room, feeling almost like a stranger. Why did going home always make her feel lonely? She had happy memories of her childhood there, with her mother alive and Horus's mother, Tentamun, as a maid. But after Seshta's mother died and her father remarried, home just didn't feel like home anymore. Anyway, she'd lived in the temple for five years now.

She went out the back of the house and greeted a few servants tending horses outside the stables. She did a series of cartwheels across the yard, just to keep her muscles loose. When she landed by the kitchen doorway, she felt lighter. She didn't need to mourn this home when she had another one to visit, one full of happiness and love.

She chatted with the cook and got two loaves of fine wheat bread. Back in the courtyard she called to one of the stable hands. "Pawero, can you help me?"

He came toward her, smiling and wiping his hands on his kilt. "Of course, Miss Seshta."

She led the way up the stairs to the roof, where the servants slept in hot weather.

"Hold these, please." She handed Pawero the bread and sat on the edge of the roof. Seshta turned and lowered herself until she hung from the roof's edge by her hands. Then she dropped to the ground. She landed with knees bent, caught her balance, and reached up. Pawero handed the bread down to her, his eyes twinkling. "Will you be needing me again, or will you use the front gate when you return?"

She grinned up at him. "I'll manage somehow. Thank you." She turned down the alley, already focused on Reya again.

Chapter 4

Seshta trotted through the dust with a loaf of bread under each arm. Her home might not feel like home anymore, but at least she still had Horus and his family. Maybe Reya would be there, too. If not, she and Horus would go find him. They were her real family, even if they didn't share blood.

She walked a few blocks to a much poorer neighborhood. Small houses slumped together along a street too narrow for chariots to pass. Seshta shifted one of the loaves of bread so she could rap on a plain wooden door.

The door opened to reveal a six-year-old girl. Her milky blue eyes stared, unseeing, past Seshta, but her nose twitched and she grinned.

"It's Seshta. You smell like incense."

"Clever child." Seshta bent down to kiss her cheek. "And what else do you smell?"

Webkhet inhaled deeply. "Bread! Made with light flour... and a bit of honey."

Seshta laughed and gave her the loaves. "Let's take them in to your mother."

Horus grabbed his sister from behind and picked her up. "Is that fresh bread? Don't stand there, mouse, let her in." He carried Webkhet, squirming and giggling, across the room.

Their mother, Tentamun, bustled in from their tiny courtyard. "Oh, Seshta, darling! Horus thought you might come."

Seshta returned her hug and kiss. She gestured at the bread. "A gift from my household."

Tentamun beamed. "It's so kind of your father to remember me after all this time."

"Of course we remember you fondly! Many of the servants still ask about you." Tentamun wouldn't accept the gift if she thought it was charity from a child.

Tentamun sighed. "I do miss working there. But when your father remarried I couldn't imagine working for a different mistress, and Webkhet needed so much attention when her eyes started failing."

"We understand," Seshta said. "I'm just glad I can still see you."

"As welcome as if you were my own daughter."

Seshta gazed at Tentamun's rounded face with its deep smile grooves. Horus and Webkhet wrestled playfully. A sleek cat with mottled brown fur rubbed against Seshta's ankles. This was how a home should feel.

If she won the contest, she could earn good money and move Horus's family into a bigger house. They could all live together, with servants to wait on them, and Tentamun wouldn't look so stooped and stiff from hard work.

Tentamun asked, "Will Reya come today, too, do you think?"

Seshta and Horus exchanged glances. "I don't know," Seshta said. "We haven't seen him in a couple of days."

Tentamun sighed. "I suppose the army keeps him busy. Such a dear boy!"

"He's trapped," Webkhet said.

"What?" Horus released her, and they all turned to stare.

"I dreamed about him." Webkhet's pale eyes filled with tears. "He was alone, trapped, in a small place. He was angry... and scared."

Tentamun said briskly, "Darling, you mustn't worry about Reya. He can take care of himself."

"Of course." Horus put an arm around his sister. "He's not even on patrol, he's right here in Waset." But his eyes looked troubled as they met Seshta's.

"But I *saw* him!" Webkhet said.

Seshta touched her shoulder gently. "Perhaps it's just part of his training. You remember him talking about it? They make him do all sorts of strange things, and, of course, sometimes even Reya gets nervous."

Webkhet nodded, but her lips turned down and trembled.

Tentamun said, "Come, Webkhet, and stir the soup for me."

Mother and daughter went out to the courtyard. Horus motioned Seshta up the ladder onto the roof. They sat with their legs dangling over the edge, looking out at the city in the sunshine. Everything looked so peaceful, so normal. Seshta found it hard to believe in sinister plots while Ra caressed her face with his warmth. But who knew what dangers lurked in dark alleys or hid away in shadowy buildings? Her spine prickled.

"What do you think?" Horus asked.

"Reya really is in trouble. Webkhet has been right before when she's seen things in her dreams."

"Yes, but sometimes she gets the picture right and the meaning wrong. Remember when she saw a monster killing a white bird, and we thought it was a terrible prophecy? Then that big dog got in the yard and killed a chicken. Webkhet had never seen a dog, so she didn't know what her dream monster was. Unless we go to a priest and pay him to interpret the dream, we can't know what it really means."

Seshta jumped up and paced the rooftop. "We could do that, but Reya said he had a big secret. I'm not sure we should tell anyone anything that might expose him." She did a handstand, took a few steps on her hands, and turned so she could see Horus.

He winced. "Do you have to do that up here?"

Seshta dropped to her feet and sat beside him. "I'm scared! He said he'd be at the river two days ago, and we haven't heard a word from him. That's not like Reya."

"Isn't it?"

Seshta smiled reluctantly. "All right, he's not the most reliable person. But after his dark hints that day, I really am worried."

She took a deep breath. "I've been having dreams too."

Horus shot her a startled glance. "Like Webkhet's, you mean? Why didn't you say anything?"

"Yesterday, I didn't want to worry you. And I didn't know what it meant. But I had another dream last night. It was awful." She remembered her mother's statue, but she wasn't ready to share that, even with Horus. "We need to find him."

"You make it sound so easy. What are we supposed to do?"

"Well... he should be at the barracks."

"We can't go into the army camp!"

"Why not?"

Horus stared at her and shook his head. "Civilians don't just wander around in there."

"We won't wander, we'll ask for Reya."

"And say what, 'Can Reya come out and play?' That will help his career. If he's not in trouble now, he will be when a couple of kids come asking for him."

Seshta waved a hand impatiently. "Don't be silly. We'll say it's an emergency, and we have a message for him. We'll say his mother is sick."

"What if they don't let us talk to him alone? He'll think she really is sick!"

Seshta closed her eyes and watched the bright sunspots dance behind her lids. "All right... we'll say his sister is sick. Since he doesn't have one, he'll know it's not true."

"They might know he doesn't have a sister. Or he might think we're talking about Webkhet, and—"

Seshta opened her eyes and glared at him. "Do you have a better idea?"

Horus sighed. "No."

Seshta lay back and put her hands over her eyes. "All right, then. After lunch, if Reya hasn't come, we go find him."

They ate vegetable soup and bread. Seshta tried to answer Tentamun's questions about temple life cheerfully, but she couldn't keep from fidgeting and glancing toward the door. As soon as they had cleaned their bowls, Seshta and Horus said goodbye.

"Off to the river again?" Tentamun said. "I swear, you children spend more time there than in your own homes."

"Can I come?" Webkhet asked.

"Not this time, mouse." Horus gave her a pinch. "You might fall in."

She pouted. "I won't! I'll sit on the dock and I won't even move!"

Seshta bent to kiss her cheek. "Next time, I promise. We're going too far today for your little legs."

Webkhet started to protest, but Tentamun hushed her. "I need you today. Perhaps Horus will bring us some fish tonight, so we should go to the market and get a few vegetables to go with it. You're so good at picking out the best ones."

Horus shot Seshta a guilty look and she shrugged. They hadn't actually lied. Tentamun need never know that she had assumed wrong, if only Horus could keep his face innocent.

They hurried down the dusty alley and turned onto a street broad enough for a dozen chariots to drive side by side. They passed crowds of people and

Seshta scanned them, half expecting to see Reya's grinning face.

Some people wore sparkling white linen clothes and glossy wigs with hundreds of braids. Others wore coarse-woven kilts or dresses, with roughly cut hair or shaved scalps. Donkeys pulled carts. Rich young men drove their chariots fast, scattering the crowds. Four muscular, dark-skinned Nubians carried a litter with a reclining woman peeking out from behind gauzy curtains. Peddlers sat beside baskets of food or other goods. But Seshta didn't see Reya.

Seshta and Horus passed a temple to the creator god Ptah and turned down a long dirt road. The sun beat down and their pace slowed as they neared the walled barracks.

Horus wiped a hand over his shaved head and flicked away the sweat. "We're here. Now what?"

Seshta wasn't sure if the sweat drenching her sides was due to the heat or her anxiety—her fear of finding out that something terrible had happened to Reya, her fear of finding out nothing at all.

She tossed her head and said a quick prayer to Hathor. "Now we go in."

Chapter 5

A stocky man with a stubble of graying hair stood in the wedge of shade by the entrance, a long spear held in one hand. Only his eyes moved as they approached, scanning them from head to feet.

Seshta wished she'd worn some expensive jewelry and her good wig instead of this simple, short one. She would have looked older, as well as more important. With her fine linen dress gray with dust, she looked like a grimy child.

She had to improvise, like she often did when dancing. She smiled and bowed, as if he were the one of higher rank. "Greetings, oh exalted warrior, spear-bearer for Pharaoh and Amun. Many blessings upon you this fine day."

The guard just watched her.

Seshta hurried on. "Many apologies, sir, for interrupting you in your important duties, but we come with a message for one of your soldiers. We would not presume to disturb you, but it is vital that we speak to him at once."

The guard shifted his weight. "Who's the man, and what's the message?"

Seshta took a breath. "The soldier's name is Reya, son of Bemenamun, a young man of this city, with your battalion only a year. The message we would prefer to deliver in person, for it concerns an illness in his family, and the news would come gentler if heard from us."

She held her breath as he stared at her. Horus stood silent at her side, fingering the amulet around his neck.

The guard turned his head and called to someone inside the walls. "Harwerre! You know young Reya of Waset? Is he about?"

A voice answered. "Haven't seen him in a couple of days. I heard a rumor he deserted."

Seshta bristled. "That's nonsense!"

The guard scratched his head. "That can't be right, or they would have sent us to find him. There's a girl here with a message for him. Can you take her in and ask the men in his unit?"

He gestured with his head, and Seshta scurried through the gates with Horus close behind. A sun-bronzed young soldier greeted them. "This way. You came at a good time; that unit is resting inside after training drills. Someone will know about your friend, if he isn't there himself."

"I'm sure he didn't desert," Seshta said.

The soldier glanced down at her. "Of course not. It was just a rumor, and I'm sure it's wrong." He grinned. "We all dream of deserting, and that's why we talk about it."

Seshta nodded, but she couldn't shake her anxiety. A rumor like that wouldn't get started if Reya were here to prove it wrong.

They crossed a dusty courtyard under a sun so bright that Seshta had to squint against the glare. The soldier led them to a low, mud-brick building and stuck his head inside. Seshta shaded her eyes and tried to peer past him, but she couldn't see anything in the dim interior.

"Hey!" Harwerre called. "Where's Reya?"

The voices drifted out. "He's off on a mission to Nubia, isn't he?"

"No, he went north, to the delta."

A gravely voice growled, "Don't know why that young pup got picked for the job. Hardly knows his sword from his nose."

"Well, it was a punishment, wasn't it? Would you want to be tramping through this heat?"

"No, he's on a secret spy mission," a shrill young voice insisted. "He was talking to the commander, and then he just went, without a word to any of us."

"I saw him get into a chariot," someone drawled. "At night it was, so I couldn't see who he was with, but that doesn't sound like punishment, going off in a chariot."

"If it was so dark you couldn't see who he was with, how can you be sure it was Reya?"

Harwerre broke through the din. "So none of you actually knows where Reya is?"

The voices babbled again. "I tell you, he's—"

Harwerre turned to Seshta and Horus, frowning and shaking his head. "I'm sorry. They're no help at all, except obviously Reya isn't here."

Seshta swallowed and managed to whisper, "Can you find out how long he's been gone?"

Harwerre stuck his head back in the room. "Hey! When did he disappear?"

Seshta trembled. Disappear. Maybe Reya was just off on a special mission, but shouldn't someone know? To just disappear....

The soldiers finally agreed that Reya had last been seen two days before. He'd been with them during drills and then had gone off during afternoon break. Seshta's hands clenched. That was when he'd come to see them at the river. When he'd had his big secret and his hints about meeting royalty and not going back to the desert with the troops. He'd been back at the barracks in the evening, the soldiers agreed, but he hadn't slept there that night.

The sweat dripping down Seshta's neck felt cold. Horus squeezed the amulet around his neck, his face tight.

Harwerre turned with a shrug. "That's all we'll get here. I'm sorry."

Seshta stared at him, trying to think of anything to say. That couldn't be all! "Can't we ask someone else? Who's in charge?"

Harwerre's face softened in sympathy. "All right, if anyone knows, the commanders will. They won't like being disturbed, but we can ask."

"Oh, could you?" Seshta swayed, her legs suddenly weak. She gave Harwerre a shaky smile. "You're very kind."

He smiled back. "I may get a beating for this, but it wouldn't be the first one. I can see you're worried. I wouldn't want my little sister worrying about me."

Harwerre led them across the dusty courtyard under the beating sun. Seshta's dress stuck to her body, and she knew the dark kohl around her eyes must be running. She rubbed her fingers under her eyes, hoping that would remove the black streaks, not make them worse. The heat rose up in shimmering waves from the pale ground, making her head throb.

She shaded her eyes as they turned a corner. She hadn't even noticed the noise until they were upon it. Swords clanged as dozens of young men rushed at each other. Dust billowed up from their feet and made muddy rivulets down their sweaty bodies. One skinny boy, tanned dark as a farmer, swayed at the edge of the group. His sword dropped to the ground, his knees buckled, and he landed on hands and knees, head drooping forward. An older man, broad as a door and all muscle, strode forward and hauled the boy up by his shoulder.

"On your feet! Do you think we fight only in cool weather, when it's convenient? You'd better toughen up if you want to survive the battlefield." He peered into the boy's face, then gave him a shove that sent him staggering toward the wall. "Get some water— just a mouthful—and I want to see you back fighting."

Seshta recoiled as the man glanced their way and scowled. He stomped toward them with a strange rocking gait, as if his bulging thigh muscles kept him from walking with his feet close together. He stood spread-legged in front of them, hands on hips. Seshta stared at the scars running down his arms and zigzagging across his chest. Even his face and neck were marred by ropy scars, and his left ear was missing.

"What are these... civilians... doing here?" He made "civilians" sound like the worst insult.

Seshta glanced at Harwerre and could see the tension in him, as if he wanted to step back but didn't dare. He stared somewhere over the scarred man's shoulder and spoke loudly. "General Kha'i! Sorry to interrupt training, sir! These civilians have an important message for recruit Reya of Waset. Do you know his whereabouts, sir?"

The general studied Seshta with a look of disgust. Her face burned, but she forced herself to remain still. Horus hid behind Harwerre, strangling his amulet with a trembling hand.

"Friends of Reya, eh?" General Kha'i made that, too, sound like an insult. He smiled, but it wasn't friendly. "Reya is not here. Nor should you be. This is no safe place for little girls." He took a quick step sideways so he could see Horus, who shied back like a skittish horse. "And young men should never come to the barracks unless they are ready to volunteer!"

General Kha'i strode away, calling over his shoulder, "Get them out of here!"

Harwerre grabbed Seshta and Horus by the arms and dragged them back around the corner. Once out of sight, they paused, and each took a deep breath.

Harwerre gave them a shaky smile. "Well, that could have been worse. I didn't get a beating, and you, friend," he tapped Horus on the chest, "aren't a soldier. Hide if the recruits come calling!" He started walking across the courtyard. "This is no life for civilized people."

"Who was that man?" Seshta asked.

"General Kha'i is in charge of new recruits. He's survived more battles than just about anyone, and he's as tough as they come. His training will help keep you alive—if it doesn't kill you."

Seshta shuddered. To think that she had complained about the priestess's scolding! And Reya had been living with this for a year.

"But what about Reya?" she wailed. "We don't know anything, except he seems to have vanished!"

Harwerre shrugged. "I don't know. Maybe he really did run away. He's not dead, at least, or they would tell you."

Seshta couldn't believe it. Reya wouldn't run away, and he couldn't just disappear for no reason. "I won't leave!" She heard her voice go high and shrill. "I won't go until we find Reya."

A voice came from behind them. "Who's looking for Reya?"

Chapter 6

They turned and peered through a dark doorway. Seshta could barely make out the shadowy figure seated at a desk inside. Harwerre straightened and saluted, but he was smiling, with none of the tension from his encounter with General Kha'i. "General Menna, sir! Yes, sir, these young people have an important message for Reya of Waset, but no one seems to know where he is."

"Come inside."

Seshta's heart beat fast, hope rising in her as they stepped into the dark room. Seshta blinked away the lingering sunspots and scanned the small office. It hardly looked like an army barracks, with colorful linen hangings on the walls and reed mats on the floor. Behind a wooden desk sat a lean man, perhaps forty, with a smooth-shaved head and a polite smile. "What is your relationship to Reya?"

Seshta's shoulders had knotted with tension during the confrontation with General Kha'i. Now they relaxed. She could handle this man, polite and refined like one of the priests and obviously someone powerful, who could tell her the truth about Reya.

Horus hovered in the doorway, silent, as Seshta stepped forward and bowed. "We are old friends—the brother and sister of his heart. One of his family is sick, perhaps dying, and we thought he should know." She held her breath, wondering if he would ask which family member, wondering if he knew anything about Reya's home life.

"And you could not find him." General Menna clucked his tongue and looked at Harwerre. "You should have come to me first."

"I would have, sir, but I thought you were still in the north."

"I returned late last night. I suppose you asked General Kha'i? What did he tell you?"

"He... gave us no information, sir."

"No, I suppose he wouldn't." General Menna smiled. "You must have been worried. Well, there's no need. I shouldn't tell you this either, but young Reya is on a special mission for Kha'i. I can't give you any details, but I expect he'll be back in a week or so. I'll give him your message and see that he gets a few days off to visit home."

Horus said, "Why Reya?"

They all looked at him, and he stepped back, stammering. "I mean, he's so young. He's only been a soldier for a year...."

"But he shows great promise," General Menna said. "Why Kha'i chose him for this mission I do not know, but I imagine Reya volunteered."

Seshta said, "Against the Libu?"

General Menna's gaze jerked toward her. "What do you know about the Libu?"

She blushed. "Nothing. It's just something he said. Just the name, really. I don't know any more."

General Menna stared at her a moment, then rearranged some clay tablets on his desk. "Well, that's all I can tell you, I'm afraid." He glanced up. "I'll give young Reya your message. What are your names?"

"Seshta, daughter of Thanuro, and this is Horus, son of Hor-mose. Thank you. You've been very kind." She and Horus hurried outside, while Harwerre exchanged a few more words with the general.

"Why did you mention the Libu?" Horus hissed.

"I don't know! It just came out. Why did you ask him why they chose Reya? Do you think we got him in trouble?"

Horus shrugged. "I don't know what to think. I just want to get out of here before I'm recruited."

Harwerre escorted them to the gate. They thanked him and the guard and hurried away. At the end of the street they paused, pressing into the sliver of shade along a wall. Seshta's head still throbbed from the heat and the tension.

Horus sighed. "I'm glad that's over."

"Me, too. But we didn't get to see Reya."

"No, but at least we know where he is, sort of. And if Reya actually volunteered for this mission, it can't be too bad." Horus leaned against the wall and closed his eyes. Sweat glistened on his forehead and along his nose. "Anyway, there's nothing more we can do. Let's go to the river and swim."

Seshta stared back toward the barracks gate. "I just wish...."

"What?"

Seshta shivered despite the heat. "I don't know. I don't like that General Kha'i. If he sent Reya somewhere, I bet it is dangerous. And I bet it wouldn't matter whether Reya wanted to go or not."

Horus frowned. "He didn't seem to like Reya very much."

"I'll bet he doesn't like anyone! And no one likes him. Harwerre was scared of him, and even General Menna didn't like Kha'i."

"Maybe, but that doesn't mean anything... does it?"

Seshta pressed her hands against her eyes. "I wish I knew. We should have asked more questions, but I couldn't think of any." She took her hands away and scowled at the black streaks on them. "Oh, cow dung, my kohl is all over the place. I look awful, don't I?" She stepped into the road. "Let's get out of here and go for that swim. I can't even think straight."

Horus started to say something, but rapid hoofbeats drowned out the words.

Horus grabbed Seshta and pulled her back. She slammed against the wall and gasped as a chariot rounded the corner in a cloud of dust.

She glimpsed two black horses, sides shining with sweat. Then the wheel of the chariot flashed by a hand-span away, tugging the air from her lungs.

They pressed against the wall, choking on the dust. "He might have killed you!" Horus said.

As Seshta got her breath back, her trembling slowed, but she still tingled from her neck to the fingers of her right hand. She shook out her arm and rotated her shoulder. "It's numb. If this stiffens and hurts my dancing, I'll kill that charioteer!"

"Huh. Foreigners!" Horus glared past Seshta. She turned to look as the horses reared to a stop in front of the barracks gate. The guard stepped forward and spoke to the man in the chariot.

"It's the Libu!" Seshta hissed.

"Who?"

Seshta squinted through the glare as the dust settled. Was that the man she had seen in the market? He had the same curly beard and brown hair braided on one side. But instead of a cowhide cloak, he wore an Egyptian linen kilt and beaded broad collar. Wide gold bands flashed at his wrists. He looked something like the other man, but it was so hard to tell foreigners apart. Still, anything to do with the Libu interested her now.

The guard disappeared. The Libu—or whatever he was—looped the reins around the top bar of the wickerwork chariot and stepped off the back. Dark tattoos covered his legs.

Someone came through the barracks gate. Seshta gasped as General Kha'i clasped hands with the charioteer. The Libu gestured toward his chariot, the two men got on, and the Libu took up the reins. He flicked them and wheeled the chariot in a tight turn, headed back toward Seshta and Horus.

"Quick!" Seshta dragged Horus around the corner. She couldn't see any place to hide, so she pressed back against the wall.

"Who was that charioteer?" Horus asked. "Did you recognize him?"

"I'm not sure... but I think he was a Libu!" Her heart raced. The gods had given her another path to follow.

With a thud of hoofbeats and clattering of wheels, the chariot rounded the corner and passed them. A cloud of dust roiled behind it down the street, enveloping and blinding them.

Seshta sneezed and blinked to clear her eyes. "Come on! Let's follow them." She started to run.

"What? Are you mad?" Horus gasped out the words as he jogged behind Seshta. "We'll never keep up. What's the point, anyway?"

"I don't trust General Kha'i, and I want to know what he's doing with a Libu, if they're so dangerous!" Seshta squinted and coughed against the dust. She saw a pile of horse manure at the last moment and leaped over it.

They reached the end of the street. The clatter of hooves faded as the chariot sped away to the left. "We'll never catch them," Horus gasped.

"We have to try! For Reya."

Chapter 7

They turned down a paved street. Seshta's feet, clad only in thin sandals of woven reed, slapped against the stone.

Her heart raced. Sweat dripped into her eyes. The sound of Horus panting behind her faded, but she didn't look back.

Seshta found her stride. Her breathing and heartbeat settled into a comfortable rhythm. Energy surged through her and her *ba* soared. She felt she could do anything.

The chariot, far ahead, entered a crowded street. It didn't slow much, for a chariot meant either the military or the rich, and common people darted out of its path. Still, Seshta reached the corner in time to see the Libu turn right before a small temple.

She dodged passers-by and donkeys, then swung around the corner. Something loomed up in front of her and she skidded into it, smelling sweat. She stepped back, ready to apologize.

A large hand grabbed her arm and a low voice chuckled. "What have we here?"

Seshta sucked in a ragged breath and looked up at a grinning face missing several teeth. She winced as the hand tightened on her arm and pulled her closer to his stale breath. "You must be in a hurry to find me, honeycake."

Seshta slammed her heel down on the instep of his bare foot. As he yelped, she twisted out of his grip and darted away.

Where had the chariot gone? She opened her mouth to curse, but years of temple training stopped her, and she hurriedly turned the words into a prayer. "Please, Hathor, help me... for Reya's sake."

She slowed and stared along the crowded street. The chariot had vanished.

Men, women, and children walked briskly or paused in conversation. A small group at the next corner spoke in raised voices. "—might have killed me! Why the rich should be allowed to race through our streets like drunken princes—"

"And the driver was a foreigner," someone broke in. "One of those damn Libu. Bunch of barbarians."

They scowled down the side street. With a quick thanks to the goddess, Seshta edged past them and started running.

She paused at the next corner. Had the chariot gone straight ahead, left, or right? She had entered a residential area, with no helpful onlookers to answer questions. She peered down the unpaved side streets, but she saw no cloud of dust, no fresh wheel marks in the dirt. She trotted forward, scanning the ground for signs of passage.

At the next intersection, the side streets were paved between high, blank walls. Seshta paused, studying her choices. She didn't see any clue to the chariot's path.

Seshta took deep breaths and let her heart slow. She couldn't just race through the city randomly. She had to think.

She raised her right foot, grabbed her ankle, and straightened her leg to stretch her tight muscles. The chariot must have left some sign of its path. She just had to spot it.

She switched legs to stretch the other one. Should she jog along the road, looking for wheel marks at each side street, or actually go down the side streets as she went along? Or wait for the chariot to return?

She heard a faint sound and spotted a child peeking out of a doorway, watching her. Seshta dropped her foot and walked closer. "Did you see a chariot pass here?"

The little girl stared up with wide, dark eyes.

Seshta fought down her impatience and crouched to be nearer the girl's height. "A chariot with two black horses? Did you see the pretty horses?"

After a moment, the child nodded.

"Such pretty horses! Which way did they go?"

The girl tilted her head to one side, gazing at Seshta. She pointed down the street to the left.

"Thank you!" Seshta sprang up and dashed off. Soon she heard the whinny of horses ahead, but, of course, the city held more horses than just that black pair. Still, what could she do but go forward? The chariot must be close, or why would they have turned into this quiet, residential neighborhood at the edge of the city?

Unless they knew she was following, and they were trying to lose her.

Seshta laughed and scolded herself for such a foolish thought. If a brute like General Kha'i wanted to get rid of her, he wouldn't run and hide. He'd throw her in prison or knock her down. Anyway, how could he know she'd chased him?

She slowed to a walk, tired from the heat and sticky with sweat. Her feet hurt where her sandals rubbed between her toes. She thought longingly of the river and wondered where Horus was.

A man's laugh came from behind the high wall to her right. She stopped to listen. Voices rumbled, but she couldn't hear what they said. A few paces ahead, a guard stood between the pillars of a tall gateway, with his back to the street. Seshta crept past, glancing sideways through the entrance.

Her heart soared. A groom was unhooking the second black horse from a painted chariot.

Seshta hurried past before anyone noticed her. She had to find out more about that place, but how?

She must look a mess in her dusty dress, her kohl-smeared face flushed from running. A child might answer her questions, but a guard would shoo her away.

At the end of the street, the paved path sloped downward to the glittering waters of the Nile. A fig tree rose above the wall to her left; a few of its fruits lay on the path in sticky blobs. Behind the walls must lie the riverside gardens of the rich.

Seshta peered around the end of the walls. Along the bank a few small boats bobbed against their moorings. The scent of roses and jasmine drifted on the breeze. Across the river, fields of golden wheat stretched into the distance. A dozen brown-backed workers bent among the grain, too far away to notice Seshta.

The river dazzled her eyes with reflections and lured her with its promise of cleansing. She wasn't sure what to do next, but any problem looked easier when you were clean.

She pulled off her dress and dropped it on the ground, set her wig on top of it, and slid into the water.

Seshta scrubbed the dust off her skin and carefully washed around her eyes to remove the smeared kohl. The cool water felt like the breath of life. She wished Horus were there to enjoy it. And Reya, too, of course, laughing and splashing and trying to dunk her. She closed her eyes and imagined the scene. Would they ever swim together again?

She perched on the stone steps and thought about what to do next. She couldn't risk going into the estate, because General Kha'i might see her. She had to charm the guard to get what information she could. She wanted to make a good impression, so she dunked her dress in the river and rinsed out the dust.

She pulled on the wet dress and slapped the dust from her wig. Her dress stuck to her skin and water dripped from the hem onto her feet. She plucked a dangling fig and munched on it while she let the sun dry her. The sweet fig removed the stale, dusty taste from her mouth.

Seshta washed the fig's stickiness from her hands and then turned back up the street. She couldn't wait for the sun to finish drying her dress. At least the fine linen would show her status and even a guard would be polite to a young woman of good family. Thank the Goddess he was Egyptian and not some foreigner with poor manners.

The chariot and horses had disappeared and the guard stood alone in the gateway. Seshta smiled at him. "Good afternoon. It's terribly hot today, isn't it?"

He smiled back. "Miserable. You look damp. Have you been for a swim?"

"You're very observant! Just don't tell my mother. She sent me on an errand, but I had to cool off first."

"In this sun, you'll be dry before you get home."

Seshta edged closer and saw a tree-lined path leading to a building painted in the Egyptian style. "What a lovely estate. I bet it has a wonderful garden. It's too bad you have to be out here, instead of resting by the river."

He laughed. "You're right, the garden is really something, but I seldom see it even when I'm not on duty."

Seshta pouted sympathetically. "Your master isn't very kind, then. All for him and nothing for you?"

The guard glanced back over his shoulder before answering. "That's him, all right. I tell you, I don't much like working for a foreigner."

"A foreigner!" Seshta gasped. "What is he, Mittani?"

"No, Libu. He has a lot of his own men here, too, as bodyguards and such." He glanced back again, then leaned toward her and whispered, "They're different, you know. Strange habits. Not like us."

Seshta opened her eyes wide. "How do you stand it? Why do you stay?" Without the dark kohl to draw the sun's rays away from her eyes, the dazzling light hurt, and she blinked.

"Well, the pay is good, I'll admit that. And he treats people all right. Plenty to eat and no beatings. If he weren't foreign, he'd be a fine master. They're just strange, you know? They don't bathe properly. The master keeps clean, but a swim in the river is enough for his men."

Seshta wrinkled her nose. "What's he doing here, anyway? I suppose he's a merchant?"

"Horses. One of the biggest horse traders in the city. Brings them from his homeland and breeds some here as well. Fine animals they are, too. Even the royal palace buys from him!"

They both jumped at a noise from beyond the trees. The guard whispered, "Someone's coming. You'd better go."

Seshta smiled and murmured, "Blessings." She walked down the street, trying not to hurry too much. If General Kha'i came out, would he recognize her? She wouldn't let herself look back, though she desperately wanted to do so.

As she turned the corner, she finally glanced back. The street lay empty. Seshta sighed and kept going. Now what? Find Horus, first of all. Where was that main street?

She paused. She had better make sure she remembered how to get back here! She wouldn't want to lose the place, after the trouble she'd taken to find it. Too bad she hadn't had a chance to ask for the horse merchant's name. Seshta studied the buildings, making sure she knew where to turn as she retraced her path. Soon she reached the busy market street and scanned the crowd.

Half a block away she spotted Horus talking to a woman carrying a basket. The woman shook her head, and Horus turned away. As Seshta came up behind him, he asked a thin boy, "Did you see a girl run past here? Running fast, like the wind?"

"No." The boy looked over Horus's shoulder at Seshta. She grinned and winked at him.

"Perhaps I can help," she said.

Horus whirled. "Oh! I've been looking everywhere for you. You know I sit in a workshop all day. I can't keep up with you."

"It's all right. Let's go."

They started down the street. "You lost them, too?" Horus asked.

"No, I found them." She glanced at Horus. His lips were cracked; muddy sweat drenched his face and chest; his feet dragged in the dust. "You look thirsty." She stopped at a stall selling grape juice and traded a bead from her bracelet for two cups.

Horus drained his drink. He smiled a little, though his eyes still looked dull. "Now what?"

Seshta pondered. General Kha'i and the Libu weren't going to stand next to the wall and shout their plans. She needed time to think, and Horus looked ready to drop.

She gave him the rest of her drink. "Now we head to the river for a swim, and I'll tell you what I found."

By the time they finished swimming, the Sun God was racing his chariot toward the western horizon. They strolled to Seshta's house, enjoying the cool evening breeze on their damp skin.

"Father will expect me to stay here for dinner," she said. "Come in and get some fish to take home for your mother."

Horus nodded. "I hope they won't want to hear how I caught them."

She glanced at Horus's half-closed eyes. "Just tell them you had a long day and you're too tired to talk. They'll believe that."

Seshta paused to speak with the gatekeeper. "Those girls—what happened with them?"

Nebra grinned. "Oh, miss! You wouldn't believe it. I thought I had them all under control, and then that cute little one—"

"Miw, we call her."

His smile widened. "Miw, like a little cat. A good name for her. I'm here trying to hold onto the others, and then she comes walking back from the house saying you're gone. I never even saw her slip away." He shook his head in admiration. "She's two handfuls, that one."

"Hmm. Yes."

"Oh, miss, I'm sorry, but I thought since you were gone anyway, it didn't matter much."

"It's all right, Nebra. Miw is two handfuls." She would have to watch out for Miw. Until she knew Reya's secret, and how best to help him, she didn't want to attract the attention of the Eyes and Ears of Pharaoh. On the other hand, Miw probably could have gotten into the Libu's estate. If only Seshta dared ask for Miw's help!

They headed for the kitchen where the cook gave Horus two nice perch. Seshta sent him on his way and wandered back to the house. She went to her room, though it hardly felt like hers anymore. All her childhood things sat still and lifeless, unused and almost forgotten. It felt like stepping into a tomb, with the grave goods laid out for the afterlife. Even her mother's shrine had more life to it, with its fresh flowers and fruit.

Seshta tossed her head. Why did she have such morbid thoughts?

She was just worried about Reya. Three full days he'd been gone now. She was sure that nasty General Kha'i and the Libu were involved. She needed to find out what was going on, but how? She and Horus hadn't come up with any answers yet.

A maid slipped into the room. "Welcome, Miss Seshta. I thought I heard you come in. Would you like to bathe?"

"Yes, thank you, Neferure." She grinned. "But whatever made you think I might need a bath?"

The maid laughed. "The day you come home without dust on your feet, I'll know you've really grown up. And a sad day that will be. Come now, step into the basin and I'll pour the water. It's nice and cool."

Seshta sighed with pleasure. But her heart kept returning to Reya. She wondered what he was doing right then, angry and afraid in a small, dark place. How could she enjoy anything, without knowing that he was safe?

Chapter 8

Seshta scowled all the way back to the temple the next morning. She wanted to spend the day looking for Reya, not chanting long, formal praises to the goddess. She droned along with the others, her thoughts on Reya. Where could he be? Why hadn't he told her more that day on the river, instead of acting mysterious and important? How did General Kha'i and the Libu figure into all this? She hated to think of Reya tangling with such dangerous men.

"Honestly, Seshta," the priestess scolded, "where is your heart today? You are shaking your rattle out of beat."

Seshta glanced at the rattle, shaped like Hathor's cow head and hung with metal disks. She'd forgotten she was holding it. "I'm sorry, Mistress."

"Really, dear, we all know you are not meant for temple life, but while you are here, you must do your best. Devote all your heart to your duties until you leave us."

Seshta pressed her lips together. Her dancing honored the goddess, and that should be enough.

"Seshta?"

She sighed. "Yes, Mistress." She would try harder. Perhaps if she focused her devotions, Hathor would guide her in finding Reya.

Miw sat beside her at lunch. "You look tired. You must not have gotten much rest yesterday."

Seshta picked at her pigeon and vegetables. "If only you knew."

"Don't practice too hard, or you'll wear yourself out before the contest. And I bet Idut that you'll win."

"Thanks." She glanced up to see Sit-Hathor watching her. "I can't believe she's taking this so seriously."

"Isn't winning the contest the most important thing to you, too?"

"Yes... at least it was." She could hardly believe how simple things had seemed just a few days before. She wished she could forget everything besides dancing. But Reya filled her mind as if he stood in front of her.

"Miw, does your father know a lot of foreigners?"

"Of course. It's part of his job to keep track of them. Not every poor worker, but anyone with money or power—anyone who might be criticizing Pharaoh and stirring up feelings against him."

Seshta carefully selected an olive. She tried to sound as if she were just making conversation. "Oh? How does he know? How does he find the dangerous ones?"

Miw tilted her head to one side and studied Seshta the way a cat watches a mouse. "Lots of ways. Informers. Undercover agents. Gossip in the taverns."

"People gossip to your father?"

"No, of course not. Anyway, the foreigners have their own favorite taverns. The Greeks go to one, the Mittani to another. Egyptians could go in, but they would be noticed. But agents go in disguise, and sometimes Father buys information from the tavern owner or the women working there. Men will say things to a woman that they would never say to a man. Why are you asking?"

"Oh, just wondering. I saw a man in the market the other day, a Libu I think.... He said some bad things about Egypt, and I wondered if he was dangerous."

"If he criticizes Egypt in public, you can be sure my father already knows about him. What did he look like?"

Seshta closed her eyes and tried to remember the man with General Kha'i. "Brown hair. A braid on one side and a long, curly beard."

"You've just described every Libu in Egypt and out of it."

Seshta scowled. "It's not my fault they all look alike!"

Miw chuckled. "No scars, no limp, no missing limbs? No unusual pattern on his cloak?"

"No cloak. He had tattoos on his legs, but he dressed like an Egyptian, a rich one, with a broad collar and gold wristbands. He drove a chariot."

"That's better. It shows he's rich and has probably been in Egypt a long time, if he's dressing like us. Are you going to eat your carrots?"

Seshta pushed the plate toward her. "I think he lives near the river, in a big estate."

Miw paused with a carrot halfway to her mouth. "Was he giving directions to his home there in the market?"

Seshta felt herself blushing. "No. But I saw him heading into the north suburbs. And someone said he was a horse trader."

"Really? That sounds like Meryey. But it's hard to imagine him being foolish enough to criticize Egypt in public."

Seshta stared. "You know him?"

"I've seen him at parties." Miw popped a piece of carrot in her mouth and chewed. "He's well known in the city. Your father probably does business with him."

Across the room, the priestess clapped her hands. "All right, girls, gather in the courtyard."

Miw said, "I wouldn't worry. If there's anything going on, I'll bet my father already knows about it."

"Of course. I was just wondering."

They began dancing. At first Seshta's feet ached as they tapped the floor, and her muscles complained when she stretched them. But soon the stiffness left and her breathing deepened. The joy of dance flooded her, and her *ba* soared.

Eyes half-closed, she spun and leaped. She arched into backbends and either kicked her legs over or tightened her stomach and stood up again. By the end of their practice session, she was sweating and smiling.

"All right girls, not bad," the priestess said. "Remember, in only two days you will be performing for Pharaoh himself and many of the court officials and priests. The girl who wins the contest will lead the procession honoring the Living God!"

They squealed and murmured. Even the girls who were less skilled could hope that maybe, just maybe, they would outdo themselves and catch Pharaoh's eye. Even if a girl didn't win, a good performance could secure her future. Some hoped a prince or lord might fall in love and marry them. A few even whispered about becoming concubines to Pharaoh himself. Others wanted to advance their careers in the temple, where they could lead festivals and perform rituals.

Miw pirouetted over. "And if you take the prize? Is it love, fame, or fortune you want?"

"Me? I just want to dance." Seshta stretched her arms up over her head, arching her back. "What about you?"

Miw laughed. "I won't find my future here in the temple. Or in some rich man's home." She gazed out over the courtyard wall. "Do you ever wish you'd been born a boy? With the extra freedom they have?"

Seshta laughed. "No. Boys don't dance."

"And dancing is everything?"

She thought of Reya. "Not everything." Tension stiffened her muscles and she hugged herself. "I wish it was."

Miw's eyebrows rose, but she didn't speak.

The girls had lost interest in spying on Seshta, with the contest so close and their own hopes rising. When Seshta left the temple, no one followed.

As she stepped past a doorway, a shadow lurched out beside her. Seshta jumped back and then relaxed when she saw who it was.

"Horus! I was just coming to find you."

"I couldn't wait. I told Sunero I wasn't feeling well, and I went to Reya's house."

"Did his mother—" Seshta glanced behind her and pulled Horus farther down the street. "What did she say?"

"She doesn't know anything. I didn't want to worry her, so I couldn't tell her what's wrong. But as far as she knows, Reya is safe at the barracks. She never knows when she'll see him, maybe not for days at a time. But she thinks he's still here in Waset."

"Now what do we do? I tried to tell my father about it last night, but he said General Kha'i is well respected by Pharaoh himself and wouldn't do wrong. If Father doesn't believe us, no one else will. We need more information."

"I'm not going back to the barracks."

"They don't know anything there anyway. Or at least, the one who knows won't tell us."

They passed the market, through the thick smells of leather and straw, roasting meat, and overripe fruit. "I wonder if General Kha'i lives at the barracks," Seshta said, "or if he has a home somewhere else in the city."

"Don't tell me you want to spy on General Kha'i! He'll have us executed—or sent to the gold mines of Nubia!"

Seshta edged past a cart piled high with melons. "All right. Maybe we should concentrate on the Libu."

Horus groaned. "How are we supposed to do that?"

"Foreigners have their own taverns. We need to find out which one the Libu go to."

"You want to go to a foreign tavern? Do you know what kind of ladies go to taverns? People will think you're—you're—"

Seshta rolled her eyes. "I'd have to go disguised, of course. We wouldn't want anyone to recognize us."

Horus shook his head. "Doesn't anything scare you?"

They reached the river and she looked down at the sun glittering on the water. "I suppose if I thought about it, I would be scared. But it's like performing—you can't think about it too much or you couldn't go on. You just say you're going to do it and be the best. Then you do it."

She turned to look at Horus. "Anyway, I'm more scared for Reya than for us. Do you think it could possibly be all right? That he really could be on a mission for General Kha'i, willingly?"

Horus took a deep breath and ran his hands over his scalp. "No. I think something is wrong."

"Me, too. If your sister is right, if he really is trapped somewhere and scared...."

"She had another dream about him last night. She woke up screaming." Horus pressed the heels of his hands against his eyes. "What do we do?"

"Well... first I need a disguise. I'll have to wear a cloak and keep it closed around me, maybe alter a wig to look more like a Libu—"

Horus shook his head. "Forget it."

"Look, you just agreed—"

"We need to do something, but that disguise will never work. *Maybe* you could pass as an Egyptian boy, but a Libu? Never."

"If the disguise is really good? It will be pretty dark in there—"

"Seshta, you don't speak Libu! How will you even know what they're saying?"

She stopped with her mouth open. Her shoulders slumped. "Oh. Right. I guess I got carried away."

Horus sat on the riverbank and leaned his elbows on his knees. "We need help."

Seshta sank down beside him, leaned out over one extended leg, and grabbed her foot. Where could they turn for help? Her father would tell her to leave matters to Pharaoh and the gods. General Menna seemed nice, but he would surely trust Kha'i over a couple of youths he'd just met.

She stretched the other leg, feeling her muscles loosen and her thoughts flow more easily. "I wish we could tell Miw."

"The girl from your temple?"

"Her father is an Eyes and Ears of Pharaoh. One of the best spies in Egypt and close to Pharaoh."

"Maybe she could get us an audience with her father."

"I'm afraid we'll make things worse. If General Kha'i knows we're after him, he might get rid of Reya before anyone can find him."

Seshta put her head to her knee and spoke through the fringe of her wig. "Anyway, who would believe us? We're young so no one will take us seriously. This Libu—did I tell you his name is Meryey? Apparently he's well known in the city. Even Pharaoh buys horses from him."

She sat up and watched Horus twist some flexible reeds together. She couldn't tell if the lines between his eyes were from concentration or worry.

He said, "Maybe we're all wrong about this. If Pharaoh respects General Kha'i and the Libu, they must be all right. Pharaoh is the Living God. Wouldn't he know if something was wrong?"

Seshta flopped onto her back and stared up at the blue sky. "I don't know! I want to think so, but if Pharaoh knew everything, he wouldn't need spies like Miw's father." She stood up. "This is useless. We have to think!" She slipped off her sandals and started tapping her feet, stepping in the intricate pattern of the Sunrise Greeting dance. She should be practicing for the contest, not chasing villains. They were wasting time.

She took a deep breath and closed her eyes, feeling the sun on her skin, the moist earth under her feet. Never rush. Each dance had its own pace, and this was no different. They had to plan before they could act.

When she opened her eyes, Horus was frowning at the little animal he had made out of reeds. "It's supposed to be a giraffe, a strange creature from Punt. I saw a carving of one."

Seshta crouched beside him. "You made the neck too long."

"It was almost as long as the body in the one I saw, but the carver must have been exaggerating. It looks ridiculous." He threw the giraffe into the river and they watched it float downstream. Horus sighed. "Any ideas?"

"The market, I guess. Everybody goes there, and everybody gossips."

"It could be a long time before we hear something useful. We could spend days wandering for nothing."

"You're right. We'll have to start the gossip ourselves."

Horus stood and brushed his hands on his kilt. "At least there's less chance I'll get drafted or executed there."

Chapter 9

Seshta approached a burly cloth merchant and said, "Excuse me, didn't I see General Kha'i here the other day with that Libu horse trader?"

"What's it to you who visits my shop?" he grunted.

Seshta gave the merchant her sweetest smile. "General Kha'i said he found the best cloth in all of Waset. I wondered if he meant here."

The merchant studied her short wig, linen dress, and the bracelet of faience beads she'd brought for barter. She'd made sure she looked respectable. "As far as I know," he said, "the general doesn't have much interest in clothes. The army supplies what he needs, and he's not married."

Seshta kept smiling, though her face felt stiff. "Oh, I must have misheard. But the Libu man, Meryey, must shop at a fine establishment like yours."

"He does, though it's no great compliment. He buys everywhere." His eyebrows drew together. "How does a little maid like you know such important men, anyway?"

"Oh, my father knows everyone." Seshta leaned forward and whispered, "I don't like that Libu, though. I heard some nasty things about him. Even that he's plotting against Egypt!"

"I wouldn't know about that." The merchant turned and began straightening some piles of fabric. "If you don't want to buy something, you'd better be on your way."

"But don't you think he's—"

"I said be on your way."

Seshta and Horus wormed through the crowd in the narrow market street. He muttered, "If we learned something, I missed it."

Seshta sighed. "This is harder than I thought. We have to find a way to get people to tell the truth about Kha'i and the Libu. Maybe if I start a story—"

"Be careful! You know the penalties for insulting Pharaoh's men."

"Meryey isn't even Egyptian," Seshta said. "I won't say anything bad about General Kha'i—I'll just give other people the chance to do that."

Horus rubbed his amulet between his fingers and said in a low voice, "If we get arrested, Mother and Webkhet will be all alone, with no one to support them."

"That won't happen." Seshta put a hand on his arm. "I promise, if anything ever happens to you, I'll take care of them. If we both get arrested, I'll make sure my father looks after them."

Horus nodded, but she could see his throat move as he swallowed.

They turned a corner. "The weapons merchants," Seshta said. "Let's find the one where I saw that Libu the other day."

They waited near his stall while he helped a customer. Seshta rose up onto her toes and balanced on one foot as she thought about what to say. She had to be bold. She had to think like a spy, sneaky and clever. Maybe she couldn't pass as a Libu, but she could still use a disguise of sorts.

When the merchant finished, Seshta strode up to him and gave a brief formal bow. "Greetings, master merchant. General Menna sent me to check on recent purchases made by General Kha'i."

Behind her Horus gasped. The merchant squinted at her. "Why would the General send you and not one of his officers?"

Seshta glanced around, stepped closer, and lowered her voice. "I am his niece. He wished these questions to be secret, even from the other officers."

Horus made a choking sound. The merchant eyed him and said, "And your companion?"

Seshta glanced at Horus, obviously lower class in his coarse kilt and bare feet. "Pay him no mind," she said. "He is my servant, totally loyal. And mute."

Horus started coughing. Seshta added, "He has a bad chest. Now, about the recent weapons purchase?"

The merchant shook his head. "These military types, always suspicious of each other. General Kha'i checks on General Menna, and then General Menna checks on General Kha'i. You'd think they'd be busy enough chasing our enemies."

So General Kha'i had been doing his own spying! Seshta smothered a smile. "There are enemies and there are enemies. Now, these weapons?"

The merchant hesitated. "If Menna wants specific details, he'll have to come here himself. But I can tell you that General Kha'i paid in advance for the large purchase made recently, and I had it delivered to the barracks three days ago. One thing I like about Kha'i, he pays promptly."

Seshta leaned closer and whispered, "Did he tell you about Reya?"

"Reya? Do you mean Reya the stone carver from Aswan? Or there's a Reya who leads one of the caravans, isn't there?"

"Never mind," Seshta said. It had been a wild chance. "What about the Libu?"

"The Libu? What about them?"

"You have been doing business with the Libu Meryey."

"Certainly, with him and with other Libu, on occasion. Mostly they prefer their own weapons, and I only carry good Egyptian weapons like you see here." He gestured at the clubs, axes, knives, bows, and slingshots. "Meryey and a few of the others like my knives, so I sell them. Nothing wrong with that."

"When was the last time Meryey came here with General Kha'i?"

"Why, they were both here last week, but not—" He stopped and squinted at her. "Say, if you're going to ask so many questions, you'd better show me General Menna's seal. I can't go talking about my customers to just anybody."

Seshta cursed silently. "Of course not; anyone can see that you're an honest, respectable man. No doubt General Menna will come himself in a day or two to ask any other questions he has. He will be most pleased with my report of your activities. Now, you said Kha'i and Meryey came to you last week? They were looking at clubs, right?"

"I really don't think...." The merchant glanced around nervously. "Why look, here they come now!"

Seshta spun around to see General Menna and General Kha'i marching up the alley. Kha'i's twisted face scowled; he looked like an angry lion on the hunt. People pressed against the walls or jumped into shops to make room for the men.

Seshta babbled, "Can't let them—him—Kha'i—see me. Don't tell—Thank you!"

Horus was tugging on her dress. They scurried away as the merchant stared after them.

Behind them General Kha'i roared, "Spies!"

Horus stumbled and grabbed Seshta's arm in a grip like a crocodile's bite. She looked wildly behind them. Kha'i was glowering at General Menna, who answered him softly. General Kha'i muttered, "Do something like that again and I'll—" His words faded as he turned into the weapons shop.

General Menna glanced their way. His eyes lingered on Seshta and then slid away.

Horus and Seshta stood for a long moment, trembling so hard they couldn't move. Finally Seshta gave a little gasp and turned. They rounded a corner and ran until the crowd hid them.

"Ra save us!" Horus panted. "That was close."

"What bad timing," Seshta said. "And we were so close to getting something from the merchant. May Sebek devour General Kha'i!"

Horus leaned against a wall and clutched his amulet. "You were lucky to get that much from the weapons dealer. He might have asked about the seal earlier." He shuddered. "Thank the gods we got away safely! I hope he doesn't think to tell General Menna about our visit. Or General Kha'i!"

Seshta shivered. "You have nothing to worry about. I'm the one who lied; you didn't say anything."

Horus smiled weakly. "How could I? I'm mute."

"But did you hear what Kha'i said? Menna must be spying on him, only he got caught. That proves Kha'i is doing something underhanded."

"So if General Menna knows about it, then what are we doing? Shouldn't we just leave it to the officials?"

"No, because Kha'i is suspicious of Menna and not of us. We might find out something important the officials miss."

Horus groaned. "I don't see how. I can't take much more of this."

Seshta took a deep breath and closed her eyes. She stood tall, as if about to start a dance, and tried to empty her whirling mind. Success came through total focus on one's goal. She had to ignore all the distractions, overcome the obstacles, and keep her heart on what really mattered. Her heart slowed.

She opened her eyes. "We have to remember Reya. We're the only ones who care about him. Even if the officials do catch Kha'i, Reya might be hurt or trapped somewhere, forgotten.... We have to find him."

Chapter 10

They wasted an hour listening to a spice seller who claimed to know everything about everybody, before they realized his stories were empty bragging. By late afternoon, they had talked to dozens of people and discovered nothing. Everyone knew of General Kha'i and respected him, or at least said they did. They agreed he was good at his job, though not friendly. A few people had seen him with the Libu, but they all assumed he was buying horses, nothing more.

People had mixed feelings about Meryey. He was a tough bargainer, but always respectful. Or he was sneaky and sly, ready to cheat you. He was the right kind of foreigner, practically Egyptian, or he tried too hard to fit in, and that was suspicious. He was well known, but no one knew him well. He was, after all, not one of them.

Horus shifted from one foot to the other and rubbed the back of his neck. "I'm tired."

Seshta brushed a fringe of wig from her face. "So am I. Let's get something to eat."

They entered a busy cookhouse that smelled of fresh bread and collapsed onto cushions along one wall. As Seshta's eyes adjusted to the dim light, she studied the other patrons.

A young man paused in the doorway, glancing around. Seshta nudged Horus and gestured toward him. "Look, there's a Libu!" She had never seen him before, but by now she recognized the braided sidelock they wore. He also had the cowhide cloak of his people, though under it he wore an Egyptian kilt. He looked about 17 or 18 and did not yet have the beard most Libu wore.

"So what are you going to do," Horus said, "accuse him of being a spy?"

Seshta glared at him. "Of course not. But maybe we can get some information from him." As the young man moved past them, she called out. "Excuse me, aren't you one of the Libu tribe?"

He turned to look at her with startling blue eyes. His skin was darker than her own, but his hair was lighter than Meryey's and almost reddish. "Yes?"

"We've been learning about your country at the temple school," Seshta said.

The young man's odd eyes widened. "They teach you about my homeland? Really?"

"Oh, yes," Seshta lied. "They say it's important for us to know about our neighbors."

"But this is wonderful! So many Egyptians treat all foreigners as barbarians. I have lived here most of my life, and still people make rude comments about me, assuming I don't understand Egyptian."

"That's terrible!" Seshta said. "Would you like to join us? It's one thing to hear about a different culture from a local priest, but it would mean more coming from you."

"Thank you, that would be delightful." He ordered beer from a server. Seshta ordered drinks for herself and Horus, plus fruit and sweet cakes for them all.

"So tell us about your country," Seshta said.

"It is very beautiful. I have not been there often, you understand."

He spoke perfect Egyptian, with a formality few Egyptians used in casual conversation. "We moved here when I was a baby. In my homeland we had drought and famine. The different tribes there—the Meshwesh to the west, then the Libu, and the Tehenu in the east, and to the south the Temehu—they often fight when grazing land and food are scarce. I am afraid we are a very warlike people."

"Really?"

"Is that not what all you Egyptians think of us? Well, it is true, for the most part. Our land is very dry, barren, with rolling sandy hills. In a few places one can grow barley, but mostly we herd cattle and hunt. You need vast amounts of land for that, and when the population grows too large...." He shrugged. "The land cannot support too many of us, so we fight or look for new homes."

"Some of you come here."

He smiled, and Seshta couldn't help staring at those strange blue eyes. "Egypt is wonderful. With the annual floods, you always have enough to eat. Do you know that in foreign lands they say Egypt is so rich the donkeys kick up gold nuggets in the roads?"

"Is that so?" Seshta smiled pleasantly while her heart searched for the right questions. "But don't you sometimes feel jealous that Egyptians have so much, and your people have so little?"

He laughed. "I have plenty now. As I said, I have lived here for many years. I hardly know my people except for those who live in Waset."

Seshta leaned forward. "Do you know—" She stopped and sat back. She had to be subtle. "Have some pomegranate. Is the Libu community close here?"

"Yes, many are. There is a tavern where the Libu men go and a part of the market where we can get the foods of our homeland."

Seshta wondered why they hadn't found that. They had a lot to learn about being spies.

He took a piece of pomegranate and sucked on the seeds before continuing. "Though of course, like any people, we do not always agree. Some are very traditional and look down on those of us who choose to wear Egyptian clothing. My own mother has not learned to speak Egyptian, and I doubt she ever will."

He gestured to the single braid on the side of his head. "For her I wear my hair in the Libu style, and I wear the cloak she made me. It is hard, sometimes, for those who moved here as adults to feel this can ever really be their home. But if I had to move back, I would feel homesick for Egypt!"

"That must be hard," Seshta murmured. Horus sat silent beside her, eating dates and staring at the Libu. She said, "But some of your people have become successful here. For example, I understand there are some rich Libu horse traders."

"Yes, we Libu are famous for our horses." He signaled to a server, who brought him another cup of foamy beer.

"And do you work with horses?"

"No, not me. I am a scribe."

Horus choked on a date. Seshta said, "A scribe? You?"

He chuckled and thumped Horus on the back. "Is that so very strange? My father gave up much to apprentice me when I was a child. You see, since I speak Egyptian and Libu, as well as a little of the other northern languages, I am useful for recording trading agreements between the different lands."

When he stopped coughing, Horus said, "I only speak one language, and I can't read or write!"

"But he's very talented!" Seshta said. "You should see the toys he makes."

"I should like very much to see," the Libu said. "I notice that you have turned that fig into a mouse."

Horus jumped and put his hand guiltily over the fig, but Seshta saw that he had added a couple of coriander seeds for eyes and slivers of apple for ears. The fig's stem made the tail.

Seshta smiled and turned back to the Libu. "Do you know the horse trader Meryey? Our teacher mentioned him as an example of a successful Libu here in Waset."

"I know him a little, but...." He glanced around the room. "As I said, we Libu do not always agree. My father will have nothing to do with Meryey."

"Why not?"

"It is best not to talk of these things." He shrugged. "Anyway, it was a long time ago."

Seshta's heart sped. This could be the clue they needed, but she had to be careful. She smiled and opened her eyes wide. "But I really want to understand your culture. I have learned so much in talking to you already, and I would love to hear about different Libu."

"I know only rumors. I would not want to cause anyone trouble for something that may not be true."

"We wouldn't want that either! We won't tell anyone. It's just so interesting to hear your stories."

"Very well, what harm can it do? I am sure many people already know."

Seshta sat back, keeping her breathing slow though her heart raced, and nodded for him to continue.

"It was fifteen years ago, perhaps. Before your current Pharaoh took power. My family had recently moved here, and more Libu were arriving all the time. Things were very bad in our country then."

Seshta nodded and tried to look sympathetic.

"Some Egyptians did not want the Libu to come. They said we would try to take their land or their jobs, or w   l beg and be a burden on the temple grain stor   iers in the delta made many travelers turn bac   ne would sell them grain, and they even cha   Libu away from the village wells."

Seshta nodded again, wishing he would get to the point about Meryey.

"Some of the Libu were angry and jealous of the Egyptians. They thought that because Egyptians are farmers, not warriors, it would be easy to take the land they wanted. This man Meryey was already here then. He has been trading with Egypt for many years."

He looked around to be sure no one was listening, and then leaned forward. "It is said that he tried to start a rebellion within Egypt. He recruited the Libu living here and other foreigners, slaves mostly, and even some poor Egyptians who wanted more for themselves."

Horus said, "But an Egyptian would never rebel against Egypt!" He looked from the young man to Seshta. "Would they?"

"I can only tell you what I heard," the Libu said. "My father will not speak of it, but I believe Meryey approached him. My family is loyal to our new home, and my father would not help. He is still suspicious of Meryey, even after all these years."

"Yes, but what happened with the rebellion?" Seshta asked.

"Some of the Libu in the north made raids on the delta villages, but the Egyptian army drove them back. Before the rebels were organized here, the plot was discovered, and the leaders were arrested. Most were executed."

"Then why not Meryey, if he started it?"

"He convinced Pharaoh that he was innocent. Maybe he was. I gather he has behaved himself since then and regained the favor of the royal court."

"Why do they let him stay here?" Horus asked. "If there's any chance that he's an enemy of Egypt, why don't they make him leave?"

"Well, he does have the best horses." The Libu swallowed the last of his beer. "I must be going. This has been most interesting and enjoyable." He stood. "I have not even learned your names. I am Ker."

"My name is Horus."

Seshta smiled up at the Libu. "You may call me... Idut."

Ker bowed. "Horus the toymaker and Idut, a temple maiden. I hope we will meet again."

He strode to the door. Horus turned to Seshta. "Why did you tell him that?"

"We don't want him to know who we really are!"

"Why not? We probably won't ever see him again, and he's not friends with Meryey."

"That's what he says, anyway."

"You don't believe him?" Horus asked. "I thought he was nice. Imagine knowing all those languages. Do you suppose he can write in all of them?"

"Probably."

Horus picked up the last cluster of grapes. "So did we learn anything?"

Seshta leaned back and sighed. "I don't know. I should have asked him about General Kha'i. I forgot; that was stupid."

"The food was good, but I'm still hungry. It must be almost suppertime."

Seshta glanced toward the doorway. The street outside was hardly lighter than inside. "Hathor's horns, it's late! I need to get back to the temple." She jumped up. "What a wasted day."

Horus rose too. "I don't know; I thought it was interesting."

"Yes, but will anything we learned help find Reya? We can't keep doing this forever. We need to do something more. Something drastic."

Horus groaned. "Like what?"

"I don't know. Meet me tomorrow, and I'll think of something." She had to come up with a plan to find Reya—before they were too late.

Chapter 11

Seshta dashed across the temple courtyard. She skidded to a stop outside the private interior court. The head priestess stood just inside, her back to Seshta, with the other girls ranged in front of her.

Seshta pressed against the edge of the doorway, hoping the priestess would turn her head for a moment so Seshta could dart past. Maybe she hadn't yet been missed.

"It is quite an honor," the priestess said. "So exciting, although we might have wished for more warning. And the night before the contest! Hardly the time for such a thing; they might have waited until after, but still...."

Miw caught Seshta's eye and grinned.

The priestess took a deep breath and tossed her head. "You must all be on your best behavior. The honor of our temple rests upon you. Act like grown ladies. And I trust that you will not overindulge in food or wine the night before your performance for Pharaoh."

Seshta frowned. What in Ra's name was the priestess talking about?

"I will insist that you not be asked to dance," the priestess said. "You must save your spirit for the contest." She clasped her hands. "Some of you may have the honor of meeting the prince himself. He asked about my most promising girls. Seshta?"

Seshta jumped as the priestess studied the girls in front of her. Idut giggled, elbowed Sit-Hathor, and gestured toward Seshta with her head.

Seshta slipped into the room. "I am here, Mistress. I just—I had to—"

"Ah, there you are!" The priestess took Seshta's hands. "The prince asked about you especially!"

The other girls stirred and murmured. Sit-Hathor's mouth opened in outrage.

Seshta stammered, "What—what—but who?"

Miw stepped forward. "It's a great honor that Prince Penno has invited us to a party at his estate tomorrow night so that he may meet the girls who will be in the contest. You may trust, Mistress, that we will all make the temple proud." She winked at Seshta.

"But how does he know me?" Seshta asked.

"My dear, I have no idea," the priestess said. "I assume he knows your father, who has talked of you."

Seshta didn't recognize the name Penno, but Pharaoh Ramses had many brothers and sons. Certainly her father might know this prince through his business. Had her father actually talked about her—bragged about her—so that this prince wanted to meet her? She felt a flush of warmth. She always assumed her father forgot her existence the moment she left his sight.

The priestess clapped her hands twice and the murmuring stopped. "You are excused from your duties for tonight. You may practice individually and then go to bed early. Tomorrow will be a long day and the contest is the following morning, so get some extra rest."

Seshta stood in a daze until Miw touched her arm. "You were lucky," Miw said. "She was too excited to wonder where you were."

Seshta blinked. "Yes. Lucky."

"And luckier to have a prince asking about you, even before the contest. You don't know him?"

"I don't think I've ever heard of him. Have you?"

"He's Pharaoh's half-brother, son of the Pharaoh Sethnakht by a minor wife. No longer in line for the throne, but he might have had hopes once, before Ramses started having children."

"How do you know all that?"

Miw smiled. "In order to protect Pharaoh, we must know who might benefit from his removal. I can tell you every member of the royal court and their relationships to each other."

Miw turned toward the sleeping quarters. "Get some rest tonight. Like the priestess said, tomorrow will be a busy day."

Seshta had to focus on her dancing. But she couldn't forget Reya. He had been missing for three days already. Three days! Where was he? What was he suffering while she danced?

After all she and Horus had done to find him, what if he was already dead? What if they never even found out, if they had to spend the rest of their lives wondering what happened?

She tossed her head, trying to fling out the thought. He couldn't be dead. That would be too unfair.

But sometimes life was unfair. Only look at kind, talented Horus and his sweet mother, struggling to survive and provide for a blind child. Many people thought the gods determined one's station in life, so each got what he deserved. Even Horus refused to ask for more. But Seshta knew Horus, Tentamun, and Webkhet deserved better.

She wondered if Webkhet had dreamed any more about Reya.

All this thinking was getting her nowhere. She should be productive and practice her dance. Or plan how to find Reya. She had to do something! Her mind whirled and she paced the small room.

This was pointless. Seshta stopped in the middle of her room. She closed her eyes and breathed deeply. She tried to clear her mind. She would think later.

She bobbed her head, finding a rhythm. She started to sway and then to weave her arms in graceful patterns.

An image of Reya, sun-bronzed and laughing, leaped into her mind. Her lungs stopped working; her chest felt like stone except for the hammering of her heart.

She pressed her hands to her face. All right, she couldn't forget Reya. She didn't want to. So she would imagine him here with her, watching. He would sit in that corner, arms on his knees, grinning at her. And she would dance for him.

Seshta threw herself into the dance, using every inch of the small room for her leaps, backbends, and flips. She did a handstand and balanced, counting her breaths.

The door popped open. Idut looked in at her.

Upside-down, Seshta stared at Idut. "What do you want?"

"Do you have an extra kohl brush?"

"No."

Idut retreated but left the door open a crack.

Seshta dropped to her feet. She peeked out the door and saw Idut lingering in the hall. Seshta closed the door and dragged her clothing chest up against it. She couldn't believe Idut was still spying on her, looking for something to report to Sit-Hathor. Spies everywhere, even among the temple girls. She had better be more subtle than Idut if she hoped to catch General Kha'i!

Seshta collapsed onto her bed. What would she tell Horus tomorrow? Would she even see him? Would she be able to sneak away to look for Reya? If not, could she send Horus alone? What if he got into trouble or he disappeared, too?

She couldn't bear that. At least Reya looked for the trouble he found; Horus only followed their lead.

She couldn't abuse his friendship by sending him alone into danger.

At the back of her mind, a thought nagged her about the party. The invitation had come too suddenly, it didn't make sense, something was wrong.

But what?

Seshta woke with a gasp, her throat dry and aching. She stared at the ceiling until the world settled back into place. Voices murmured outside, girls greeting each other with excitement. The morning bell must have woken her.

She felt shaky and weak, as if she'd been sick. She had a vague memory of bad dreams, of chasing or being chased, but she couldn't remember enough to guess at the meaning.

Seshta pulled on her shift and hurried across the courtyard to the temple. Only priests could enter the inner sanctuary, but a painted stone statue of Hathor stood in the outer room. Seshta knelt in front of the goddess and prayed.

"Please, great goddess, help me find Reya. Guide me and help me to avoid every danger, not just for myself but for Reya and Horus, for all of us."

She left the temple feeling calm again. Surely the goddess would watch over such a worthy cause as theirs. Seshta didn't yet know what to do, but the answers would come to her.

Miw was kneeling by the small pool in the courtyard. She didn't look up until Seshta drew close.

"Good wishes this morning," Miw said. "Are you prepared for today?"

Seshta studied her. She could tell Miw. She could ask for help. Miw would tell her father. But would the Eyes and Ears of Pharaoh believe her? Would he care about one missing soldier? Or would he just talk to General Kha'i and believe whatever the General said?

Miw watched Seshta with a quiet smile. Her presence was a sign from the goddess. Seshta would tell her.

A gray cat stalked across the courtyard between them. It stopped by a column and mewed. Seshta stared at the fold of white dress showing behind the column. Idut peeked around the edge and then pulled back quickly. Seshta looked down at Miw, who turned, scowling, toward Idut.

Was Miw still spying on Seshta for the contest? Or hadn't she known that Idut was there?

Seshta didn't know what to think, but her trust had fled. The cat was a sign from the goddess, revealing a spy. A warning to trust no one. Feeling numb, Seshta walked out of the courtyard.

Chapter 12

The girls rushed through their religious duties, and then the head priestess crammed the day full of etiquette lessons and endless instructions. She hovered around Seshta with compliments, as if Seshta had issued the invitation herself. All the attention made Seshta's head ache and she didn't have a moment free to think.

She asked the priestess, "Do you know this Prince Penno?"

"I met him years ago, when I lived at the royal court." The priestess smoothed the black wig that made her look youthful despite the lines around her eyes. "My mother was one of the minor wives of Pharaoh Seti, of course. Prince Penno was still a youth when I entered the temple, but everyone knew him. At one time he was in line for the throne, but these things always change as new sons are born."

"Does the prince live with the royal court now?"

"No. An ambitious young man like him wouldn't lounge around at court. He became a government official and a priest of Amun. He has power here in Waset, though he's quiet about it. His patronage would be valuable for the temple and for those girls who wish to leave when their training is done."

She patted Seshta's arm. "You must think about your future. I do not think you are suited for the religious life."

"Do you think Prince Penno would help me find work as a dancer?"

"He is in an excellent position to hire you for his parties and to recommend you to his friends. Is that what you want? For me such a life would lack meaning, but I must admit that you are one of the most natural dancers I have trained."

Seshta smiled, but her stomach fluttered. She wished she had no goal this evening except to impress the prince. But her heart warned her not to forget Reya.

The sun passed overhead. Seshta knew they would get no afternoon break. It didn't seem to matter, since she hadn't come up with a plan for finding Reya. If only he would just appear, laughing about the joke he'd played on them! She could imagine his mocking grin, could almost hear his voice.

Miw sidled up and whispered, "Your friend is hanging around the entrance."

Reya!

After one wild, hopeful moment, Seshta realized Miw must mean Horus. She blinked away tears and glanced at the priestess, who was busy scolding Idut across the courtyard. "Miw, do you know where this Prince Penno lives?"

"On the south side of the temple of Amun. A huge estate, with murals painted on the outside walls." She tilted her head to one side. "I imagine many extra servants and performers will be entering through the back tonight."

"Oh? Thanks." She decided not to ask why Miw was telling her such a thing. Seshta dashed for the temple entrance.

Horus rushed toward her, fidgety and flushed. "I've been waiting for ages! I'm going to get in trouble if I keep running out on Sunero halfway through the day."

"Hush, we don't have much time. A Prince Penno has invited the temple girls to a party tonight. He asked about me especially, so I have to go."

Horus stared at her. "A prince asked about you?" He took a step back, looked at the ground, and mumbled, "Congratulations."

"Horus, stop it! I don't care about any old prince. I want to find Reya. But there's something odd about all this. I've never heard of this prince before. I can't believe my father has been bragging about me. I haven't had time to figure out what it all means, but I need you there tonight."

His eyes opened wide and he took another step back. "Me? How am I supposed to get in?"

"Pretend you're one of the hired servants. Carry dishes, or.... No, if anyone asks, show them your toys. Tell them you're supposed to make little animals and things for the guests."

He was shaking his head. "You want me to entertain royalty? I couldn't!"

"Of course you can! I bet some of them already have your toys, bought from Sunero."

Horus's eyes darted right and left as if searching for another answer. Finally he said, "I don't see how this helps Reya."

"I'm not sure either. But at least we can talk about it tonight. We can ask people about General Kha'i and the Libu." Seshta pressed her hands to her face and rubbed her eyes. "Look, I don't know what's going on, but *something* is, and I don't want to face it alone. I need you."

"Really?" Horus straightened and smiled.

"Of course! Maybe this party doesn't mean anything, but I have to go. Once I've met the prince, I can slip away. If it's crowded, no one will notice if I leave. Penno lives near Meryey—we can go there tonight."

Horus grabbed his amulet. "We'll start with the party, if I can get in. We can talk about the rest later."

Seshta gave him Miw's directions and dashed back into the temple before she could be missed. It wasn't much of a plan, but at least she had Horus.

She had a feeling that the night held secrets, and she had to reveal them to help Reya.

Chapter 13

Seshta smoothed her best fringed linen tunic and adjusted the pleated shawl that draped across one shoulder. She scratched at her bulky wig with its hundred tiny braids, a handful of them gathered together in a bunch at the back of her head. Yellow glass beads shaped like melons hung from a string around her neck and red glass studs pierced her ears. Like the other girls, her eyes were painted with dark gray kohl on the upper lids and glittering green on the lower ones.

The priestess examined the girls one by one. "You all look lovely. Now remember to—"

"Yes, Mistress!" the girls said in unison.

They piled onto litters carried by slaves. Seshta hated this form of travel—too slow and boring. But it kept their dresses clean and protected their pretty sandals, which were designed for show rather than the dusty streets.

As they passed through the city at a stately pace, people drew back to let them pass. Some bowed; others pointed and whispered. A stocky peasant woman said, "Oh! Look at the beauty in the gold necklace!" Sit-Hathor preened.

They rounded a corner at the temple of Amun and stopped in front of a tall stone arch. Bright paintings covered the walls on either side. Seshta had expected religious scenes on a priest's house. Instead she saw a chariot with rearing horses, one man driving while his companion pulled back the string of his bow. Next to them a warrior held the hair of a kneeling captive and lifted a curved sword ready to strike.

Seshta tried to ignore the tingling in her spine. Why should she be surprised at the violence on the walls? After all, Pharaoh was both the Living God and the smiter of his enemies. Many monuments showed him holding kneeling captives by the hair. The paintings meant nothing. Still, she felt glad when the gatekeeper greeted them and they entered the estate.

The priestess ushered the girls along a tree-lined path. They passed through a doorway, crossed several rooms, and finally entered the central hall. The girls crowded together so Seshta couldn't see much besides red pillars rising up to the blue ceiling. Small barred windows high on the walls let in the last of the day's light. A staircase led up, presumably to the roof, where the prince could relax on cool evenings.

"Seshta!" The priestess's voice called out from the far end of the room.

Seshta's heart jumped. She took a steadying breath, smiled, and took tiny, graceful steps forward as the other girls parted to reveal a low platform against the wall. The man seated there wore a heavy gold collar, the kind given by Pharaoh as thanks for some special deed. His handsome face had a straight nose, wide-set eyes, and golden skin that clearly had not seen long hours in the fields.

Seshta bowed as the priestess said, "Prince Penno, may I present one of our finest dancers, Seshta, daughter of Lord Thanuro."

His eyes studied her. "Welcome. I look forward to seeing you perform tomorrow."

"Thank you." Seshta waited for him to say something about her father or how else he had heard of her. She glanced at the priestess, who also seemed to be waiting. The prince said nothing more, though his lips twitched in a smile that made Seshta feel suddenly cold.

Finally the priestess said, "And another of our finest dancers, Sit-Hathor, daughter of Senenmut."

With a quick breath of relief, Seshta moved back to the other girls.

The priestess introduced each girl in turn. The prince barely glanced at most of them and said little, except when he met Miw, daughter of Lord Uben-Ra.

"Ah, yes. I know your father." He didn't smile.

Miw said sweetly, "Everyone does."

After they had finished the introductions, the prince said, "Welcome, all. You honor my house. Please proceed to the garden and make yourselves comfortable. My other guests will arrive soon."

As they filed out, the priestess murmured, "Well, he's very formal. I don't suppose he even remembers me from our days in the palace."

The scent of roses filled the garden. Ahead of them a stone pier jutted into a rectangular lake. Servants waited to pole small painted boats across the water for any guests who desired a ride. Beyond the lake, more servants waited in a pavilion, ready with wine jugs and trays of food. The shimmering sounds of a harp joined the music of bird calls. The girls separated, some to play with the lean dogs that bounded toward them, others to admire the bright fan of a peacock's tail.

Seshta wandered to the pavilion. She dipped her fingers in a silver dish of water and accepted some raisins from a naked servant girl. She glanced at the platters piled with joints of meat, bread baked into animal shapes, cheese, nuts, and fresh fruit, but she had little appetite. She wondered if Horus had gotten into the estate.

"Greetings, Mistress Idut! What a surprise and pleasure to see you here."

Seshta gaped at the young Libu, Ker. "What are you doing here?"

"Alas, I am not here as a guest, like yourself, but in my official capacity as a translator. Others from my country will attend tonight. I would be happy to introduce you to them, so you may further your knowledge of our people."

Seshta felt the color rising in her face. "Oh! We're supposed to behave ourselves tonight, and the priestess might think I'm rude to ask a lot of questions."

"As you wish. Let me know if I can be of service. Is your esteemed young friend here as well? Ah—there he is now."

Seshta turned to see Horus peering from behind a palm tree. She forced a smile. "Yes, here he is."

Horus shuffled toward them, looking as if he might skip back at any moment.

Ker said, "Greetings, Master Horus. Are you an honored guest tonight as well? Surely you are not one of the lovely temple dancers!"

"No, I—I'm working—" He shoved something into Ker's hands.

The Libu studied the little wooden hedgehog from every angle. "Remarkable! This is of your own making?"

Horus nodded. "I have more with me."

"And you share them with us tonight. A fine idea. I don't think I've heard of such entertainment at a party before. Was this Prince Penno's idea?"

"Um, no, one of the other performers invited me."

"I would love to see your other pieces."

"Perhaps later," Seshta said. "We must leave you for a moment. Nice to see you. Goodbye." She dragged Horus to a dark corner and they huddled together.

"What's he doing here?" Horus asked.

"Working, he says."

Horus wiped his forehead. "What are we going to do?"

"Ignore him. Avoid him. No. He said other Libu will be here tonight. I knew there was something odd about this party. We need to spy on them."

"But we don't speak Libu."

Seshta frowned and tugged on her earring. "Well, at least we can see who they talk to. And if they talk to anyone who's not Libu, they'll have to speak Egyptian or have Ker translate."

"What are we trying to learn?"

"I wish I knew." She paced restlessly. "Why are they here and not just meeting at Meryey's house? Why do they need Ker as a translator? Something is happening here tonight."

Seshta glanced at the garden entrance as a group of men came in. "By the lady Hathor! I was right."

Chapter 14

Horus stepped back until he hit the wall. "That's Meryey! And those men...."

"Libu, definitely. Just look at their hair and tattoos. I bet General Kha'i shows up tonight."

Horus moaned and pressed back against the wall. "We're damned."

"No, this is good. We're getting close to finding Reya, I just know it." Seshta felt energy surge through her the way it did before an important performance. She peered around a tree. "We should separate. You ask the servants about everyone. Servants know everything, and they love to gossip."

"All right. I'll talk to the servants if you worry about the general!"

"I'll meet you back here."

"Are you going to spy on Meryey?"

Seshta picked a couple of figs from the tree and juggled them in one hand while she thought. "First I'll go back to the house. Maybe I can hide in the hallway. I want to see who else Prince Penno welcomes as a guest. If they have secrets to discuss, they'll probably talk inside, not out here in the middle of the party."

"Be careful."

"You, too."

Horus clenched his amulet. "Oh, you know I will."

Seshta strolled toward the house, pretending to smell the rosebushes. When she reached the archway that led from the garden to the house, she leaned against the wall. She didn't hear any sounds from beyond the doorway, so she slipped around the corner.

A man loomed in front of her. Seshta gasped.

She blinked in the flickering torchlight and then realized his back was toward her. He held a spear and wore no wig on his shaved head. One of the prince's guards. Now Seshta remembered passing him when she'd entered the garden. Scowling, she stepped back out the doorway.

She peered around the corner at the guard. If he left for even a moment, she could dash into the next room and hide behind a column just outside the central hall.

Go away, go away, she silently commanded him.

He didn't budge. Voices came from somewhere beyond him. Seshta couldn't hear the words, but the tone was shrill, as if frightened or angry. Something was happening, and she was missing it!

She remembered the staircase in the reception hall; it would lead up to the roof. If she got to the roof, she could listen from up there.

She backed into the garden and studied the wall. The smooth plaster offered no holds, and the rooftop was twice her height. She needed Horus to give her a boost. She scanned the garden but didn't see him.

She would have to climb one of the trees that stood near the wall. Unfortunately, they were date palms, with thick trunks covered in shaggy bark that poked up in sharp spikes.

Everyone else stood at the far end of the garden, cheering as a pair of wrestlers grappled. Seshta removed her jewelry so it wouldn't jingle and wrapped it in her shawl. She slipped off her sandals, kicked them under a bush, and dropped her folded shawl on top of them. Then she pulled up her long skirt and knotted it at her hip.

Seshta glanced around. She was alone. She took two steps and put her hand on the tree.

Someone jumped on her.

She yelped as hands tore at her hair and pushed down on her head.

She put up her arms to block the blows and twisted, trying to shove her attacker away.

Seshta stumbled and sat down hard, suddenly free. Where had he gone? She couldn't see anyone.

Angry chattering came from the tree. A monkey dangled from the palm, shaking a fist at her. A jeweled collar twinkled at its neck.

Seshta let out a breath. What a fool she was, scared by a pet monkey. She would have to do better than that. "I'm sorry, but that wasn't a very polite way to introduce yourself," she whispered.

The monkey dropped to the ground, gave a screech that sounded oddly like a curse, and scampered away.

Seshta rose and brushed herself off. She studied the tree for more surprises before grabbing the trunk. She wedged her foot between one of the bark spikes and the tree and stepped up with a wince. At least the soles of her feet were hard and tough from dancing.

With a few muffled grunts, Seshta worked her way up the tree. By Hathor's horns! She had climbed trees often enough, but palms were not climbing trees. The shaggy bark offered holds, but the strips of bark wanted to peel free as soon as she put weight on them. The spikes scratched her arms and jabbed her stomach and chest. Tears sprang to her eyes. She wanted to yell or hit something.

"Ouch!" she gasped as something smacked her head. Seshta swayed and the bark started to peel away under her hand. She felt herself leaning backward, slipping away from the tree. She yelped and hugged the tree, ignoring the jabbing spikes. When the panic left her limbs, she looked up into wide, curving fronds. She had bumped a cluster of dates.

She had climbed high enough; the rooftop stood even with her knees. Now how to get across the gap?

Seshta edged around the tree. Ouch. When she stood closest to the wall, she wedged her left foot into the rough bark beneath her. Ouch. She stretched out her right leg, and her toes touched the edge of the roof. She heard a ripping sound from her dress.

Her dress had come unknotted and hung down to her knees; it kept her from stretching fully. She grabbed the base of a palm frond and stood straddled between the tree and the roof.

The tree shook as her weight pushed against it. For a wild moment she thought she was losing her grip and would plummet to the ground. She grunted, shoved off the tree, and grabbed for the edge of the roof.

Everything spun.

Seshta hit the roof with a gasp and lay groaning with one leg dangling over the edge. When the voice of her heart slowed, she pulled herself all the way up. She rubbed her arms where they prickled. She must have dozens of tiny holes all over her body. Reya owed her for this.

The rapping of hoofbeats echoed from the road. They slowed and then stopped. Seshta scrambled to her feet and dashed across the roof.

The first stars pricked the deep blue sky above. Torchlight flickered in the forecourt. Between the trees, Seshta saw several muscular men dismounting from chariots, carrying swords. Someone barked a command. Soldiers! General Kha'i must have arrived.

Seshta crept to the opening in the roof where the stairs led down to the reception room. Her breath came fast as she crouched. A bead of sweat dripped into her eye. The warm glow of lamps lit the far end of the stairwell, but most of the room lay hidden from her view.

She heard a confused sound of footsteps and murmuring. Then a booming voice announced the newcomers. "The honorable Lord Uben-Ra, the Eyes and Ears of Pharaoh, with three of his men."

Seshta gasped. Miw's father? Prince Penno had invited him? What could that mean?

Seshta held her breath. She could hear her heart beat five times in the silence. At last the Prince spoke. "Why, Lord Uben-Ra, what a surprise. You honor me with your visit. However, your timing is poor. I have guests to entertain."

"That is why I am here. My daughter is among your guests."

"You have need of her? I will send for her at once. A pity she must leave, but duty to one's father must come first."

"No need for that," Lord Uben-Ra said. "I will join her here. You are generous to offer your hospitality to the temple maidens, and I am sure a few more guests will make no difference."

Seshta wished she could see the look on the prince's face. His voice sounded sour enough. "I see. How can I possibly refuse to welcome the Eyes and Ears of Pharaoh? Khaemuast will show you to the garden, where the young ladies are. I will join you shortly, when all my guests have arrived."

"You are very kind."

Another voice said, "Right this way, sir."

The footsteps faded. Finally the prince spoke. "Is he gone?"

"Yes."

"Sekhmet take him! Why is he here?"

A man walked near the stairs, where Seshta could see him from the waist down. "It is unfortunate that his daughter is among the temple maidens. She must have informed him of the party."

"He can't know what we're doing."

"Probably he is only here because of his daughter. He may worry that you have some plans against her. We know he has been watching you for years."

Seshta's hand clenched the edge of the step. She wished she could see. She wanted to creep down the steps, but she resisted the urge, knowing that someone would probably spot her before she could see the prince.

"That may be," Prince Penno said. "Well, let him watch his daughter. Then he won't pay attention to the other girl."

Seshta drew in her breath. What other girl? Could they be talking about her?

A new pair of legs came into view, and a new voice spoke. "He is in the garden, chatting with the priestess like a regular guest. What should we do?"

"Watch him," Prince Penno said. "Keep him and his men in view at all times. Khaemuast, tell the others. Rekhmira, get to the roof so you can see the whole garden. I must speak with Meryey."

Seshta went numb. Run, her heart screamed.

Her body wouldn't respond. The legs stepped closer. The torso moved into view. Soon she would be able to see the man's head—and he would see her.

With a gasp, Seshta leaped up and stumbled across the roof. She felt as if she were swimming through honey.

She reached the edge of the roof and crouched to leap for the tree. But she hesitated, wobbling on the edge. The tree was more than an arm's length out. If she leaped for it she would stab herself on the spikes. Worse, if she didn't find holds at once, she would scrape against the rough bark as she tumbled to the ground.

She glanced back at the stairwell. She didn't have much time.

Seshta turned and lowered herself over the edge of the roof until she hung from her elbows, her legs scraping against the wall.

From the stairwell, a head rose into view.

Seshta let go and fell.

Chapter 15

A jolt shot through Seshta as her feet smacked the ground and she rolled onto her back. Her ankles ached from the impact of landing, and her breath came in jerky gasps. She lay gazing up at a dark sky swirling with lights. She blinked until finally she could focus on the scattered stars.

She groaned and sat up. She had missed the rose bushes, thank Hathor, but she had rolled onto gravel. Her back now felt as battered as her front.

The man on the roof might come to the edge at any moment. Seshta stood and took a shaky step. Her dress caught on a bush. She cursed as she tried to pull it free without ripping it to shreds. Finally she retrieved her sandals, shawl, and jewelry and scurried away from the house.

She paused under a willow tree to calm and arrange herself. She moaned as she smoothed her dress. Dust and little tears marred the fine linen, with one big rip in the hem. How would she explain the ruined dress to the priestess? She tried to cover herself with the shawl.

Most of the party guests still lingered at the far end of the garden. Musicians on lutes, reeds, and drums had joined the harpist. Seshta trudged past the pond. What should she do next? She wanted to hear what Prince Penno said to Meryey, but they would be on their guard to make sure Miw's father didn't spy on them.

Why was Miw's father there? What did the prince mean about "the other girl?" They hadn't said anything yet about Reya; she had to focus on him, whatever other strange things happened.

She saw Horus up ahead, standing between Ker and another Libu. Ker spoke while the other man nodded and studied something held in his hands. Horus stood stiffly, eyes wide, not looking at either of them. Then his gaze focused on Seshta, and his face twisted into a desperate appeal.

Seshta smiled and hurried forward. Horus didn't appear to be in danger, but he obviously wanted rescuing—

Someone hurled at her from the trees. No small monkey this time, but a body in white.

Seshta leaped away, but she landed at the edge of the pond and her delicate sandals caught in the muck. She flailed her arms to regain her balance, but the person reached out, pushing her into the pond. Seshta grabbed one of the arms and clung to it. Her stomach churned, while for a long moment they balanced, pulling on each other.

Then they both tumbled into the lake.

Seshta gulped muddy water. She kicked and squirmed, but the body pressed down on her. She couldn't get away, she couldn't breathe, she would drown.

The weight of her attacker lifted suddenly. Still blind and confused, Seshta choked on water. Her chest burned. She didn't know which way was up.

Hands grabbed her and hauled her out of the pond. They set her feet on the ground and held her shoulders while she coughed.

Seshta took a ragged breath and blinked enough muck from her eyes to see the Libu Ker.

"You!" Now he had proved his wickedness. She twisted to get away, but the sudden movement made her feel sick and weak. She swayed and would have fallen if Ker hadn't been holding her.

"It is all right, miss," he said. "She cannot hurt you now."

Seshta bent over in a fit of coughing, and Ker moved beside her, patting her lightly on the back.

She? The word finally penetrated. Seshta wiped her mouth, straightened, and looked around. Idut sat huddled under the trees a few paces away, dripping, muddy, and missing her wig.

Idut! Was she helping the Libu?

Seshta felt dizzy. Nothing made sense. She clasped her hands to her head and got another shock as she felt bare scalp. A crowd clustered around them. She must look awful: scratched and muddy, her dress torn and wig gone.

The priestess pushed through the crowd. "Oh, my dear! Are you all right?" She stopped in front of them, looked from Seshta to Ker, and put her hands on her hips. "In the name of the goddess, what happened?"

Seshta had no answer. Idut looked at the ground.

Ker spoke. "I witnessed everything, madam. This girl attacked Idut and pushed her into the water."

Seshta gaped at him. He was telling lies to get her in trouble. They were conspiring against her!

The priestess glanced around and saw Idut. "Get up, young lady. Are you all right?"

Idut nodded. One of the other girls helped her stand.

The priestess glared at Seshta. "I cannot believe you two, squabbling like children at an event like this! You are a disgrace to me, to the temple, and to yourselves."

"No, no, dear lady!" Ker said. "Idut is innocent, it was the other who attacked."

The priestess's nose twitched. "And how do you know one of the maidens of the great goddess Hathor?"

"We met earlier," Ker said. "She wished to ask me questions about my country. I must say, I was delighted to hear that you teach about the Libu in your temple schools."

Seshta felt the color rising in her cheeks. Of course—Ker thought her name was Idut. What a fool she had been. She saw Horus wedged among the crowd. He met her gaze and shrugged helplessly.

The priestess stared at Ker, eyebrows raised, then shook her head slightly. "Er... indeed. So you saw Seshta push Idut into the lake?"

"Yes, Idut walked along here and the other one— did you say Seshta?" His grip on Seshta's arm loosened as he peered at Idut.

The priestess glared at Seshta. "You, young lady, are in a great deal of trouble. I know you have been wild in the past, but attacking another girl, while a guest in a prince's home, no less! Your father will hear of this and you will be asked to leave the temple. You will not perform for Pharaoh tomorrow."

Seshta whimpered and tried to think of a way to explain.

Ker said, "No, no, my lady, you have it wrong. Idut is innocent, as I told you. It was the other girl who attacked." He gestured at Idut.

The priestess stared at him, her forehead wrinkled in confusion.

Seshta opened her mouth, but her throat felt too tight for speech. Idut stood silent, head bowed and shoulders hunched.

"Excuse me?" Horus stepped out of the crowd and bowed to the priestess. His voice trembled. "I believe there has been some confusion." He looked at Ker and said, "This young lady is called Seshta. That one—" He motioned to Idut— "is Idut."

Seshta's heart hammered in her chest. She couldn't afford questions. She had to pretend this was all an innocent misunderstanding. If only Ker would keep quiet!

Ker opened his mouth, paused, and closed it again. He looked from Seshta to Idut. "My apologies. I was mistaken." He patted Seshta's shoulder. "This lady here—whatever her name is—was the victim."

Seshta's legs went weak with relief. Maybe she would survive this night after all.

The priestess said, "Well! This is baffling as well as humiliating." She scowled at Horus. "Who are you, young man?"

Horus stammered, and the priestess said, "No, never mind, I'm confused enough. All of you, please, go about your business while I sort this out. There is no need to stand around and stare."

The crowd shifted slightly, but no one left. The other girls watched with expressions of surprise, worry, even pleasure. Prince Penno's servants and the other guests looked on with just as much curiosity. Seshta didn't see the prince or Meryey.

Just her luck. They were probably having their secret meeting while she distracted everyone by falling in the lake.

Chapter 16

The priestess stood in front of Idut with her hands on her hips. "Look at me. Did you attack Seshta?"

Idut's breath hitched. She whispered, "Yes, Mistress."

"Whatever for?"

Idut put her hands over her face and sobbed.

"I think I can answer that." Sit-Hathor stepped forward, and they all turned to look at her. Torchlight glinted off her glossy braids, white pleated dress, and gold jewelry. She looked like a princess. Seshta wanted to hide her own messy figure from the light.

"Well?" the priestess said. "Do you know something about this?"

Sit-Hathor looked at Seshta. "Earlier today, Idut said that I was sure to win the contest. I said that was not at all certain... unless Seshta had an accident tonight and twisted her ankle or something."

Several people gasped.

"I meant it as a joke, but I'm afraid Idut may have taken it seriously." Sit-Hathor's lips curved in a half-smile. "I do want to win the contest, but fairly, for my skill. It would not be a victory otherwise. Please believe me."

Seshta gazed into her eyes. Sit-Hathor was her rival and not above doing something sneaky like spying or trying to distract her, but she was also an exceptional dancer and fiercely competitive. "Yes, I feel the same way. I believe you."

Sit-Hathor asked, "Is there any way we could postpone the contest until Seshta has recovered?"

The priestess sighed. "No. No, it's impossible, with Pharaoh coming tomorrow. The procession must take place on the Holy Day; that cannot be changed. The contest must go on as scheduled tomorrow morning. Seshta, dear, are you injured?"

Seshta stretched her limbs and rotated her ankles and wrists. She hurt from head to foot, but the aches were dull, not sharp, and nothing crunched. She'd danced with worse injuries. "I'm not hurt." She glanced down at herself. "Just a mess." Her lips twitched and she held back a giggle—at least she now had an excuse for all her dirt and scrapes.

The crowd parted and Prince Penno joined them. The priestess wrung her hands and said, "My lord, please do forgive us for this outrage. I will take the girls home at once, all of them."

"That hardly seems necessary," the prince said. "I'm sure the two who suffered this unfortunate... accident... would much prefer a chance to refresh themselves. My servants will take them to the house, bathe them, and find suitable clothes. The other young ladies may continue to enjoy the party."

"I really don't think—this has been a humiliating experience, and we should go." The priestess took a deep breath. "The dance contest is tomorrow, and after her terrible ordeal, Seshta needs rest."

The sight of Prince Penno had banished Seshta's exhaustion. At the temple, she would learn nothing. But inside the prince's house.... "Please, Mistress, let us accept the prince's kind offer. I would like to remove these wet clothes as soon as possible, for fear of taking a chill."

"Oh, my! You are soaked, my dear, and that dress is ruined." The priestess hesitated and glanced at Prince Penno.

He smiled. "Please, it is no trouble at all. We must not allow my party to end in disaster. I have not even had a chance to visit with you, my dear lady, to talk of old times at the palace."

"Well...." The priestess's hands fluttered as she turned to Seshta. "If you are sure you would be happier staying? Very well then, we will stay." The crowd murmured its approval, and Seshta sighed with relief.

The priestess turned on Idut. "You, young lady, will not rejoin the party. You are in disgrace, so you will wait quietly in the house and think about what you have done."

Idut nodded, the prince gave a few commands, and servants led Seshta and Idut toward the house. Seshta gave Horus a secret smile and wink as she went. She would have a chance to be a proper spy at last. Surely she would find something to lead her to Reya.

Chapter 17

A servant led Seshta into a bathing room. The woman had thick, curly hair, black eyes, and a strong nose. Clearly not Egyptian, but not Libu either, Seshta thought. Hittite, maybe, and most likely a slave. Perhaps she could be coaxed into giving away some of her master's secrets.

Seshta needed to gain the woman's confidence, and she didn't have much time. "Have you worked for Prince Penno long?"

The woman just smiled, helped Seshta remove her clothes, and motioned toward the stone basin. Seshta stepped into the bathing area as the woman picked up a silver jug.

"Do you like it here?" Seshta asked.

The woman placed a hand on Seshta's scalp to indicate that she should lower her head. Seshta did, and murmured with pleasure as the cool water washed over her. Mud ran into the stone basin in a brown current.

"Is the prince a good master?"

The woman scrubbed her body.

"Do you have many foreign visitors? Like those Libu?"

Soon Seshta's skin shone clean from head to feet, the blood washed from her scratches. But the prince's slave hadn't spoken.

Perhaps she was deaf? Seshta grabbed the woman's arm in a damp hand and peered into her face. "Who are you? What is your name?"

The woman smiled, mumbled something, and tried to lead Seshta away from the bath.

"What did you say? What language was that? Don't you speak Egyptian at all?"

The woman dried Seshta with a towel and then gestured toward the massage table.

"No, I don't have time." Seshta tried to turn away, but the woman pulled her toward the table. "Hathor's horns," Seshta grumbled, "you don't understand a word I'm saying!" She gave up the struggle and stretched out on the table.

Had the prince sent her with a slave who spoke no Egyptian on purpose, to keep her from learning anything? Or was she worrying over nothing? Surely the prince couldn't know that she wanted to spy on him, or he wouldn't have invited her into his house.

The slave's strong hands smoothed oil over Seshta's back and then pressed deep into her muscles. Seshta grunted as the knots in her back and shoulders dissolved. She hadn't realized how sore she was. She needed this treatment if she was going to dance tomorrow.

But how could she even think of dancing? The evening was slipping away, and she'd learned nothing about Reya, or the Libu Meryey, or General Kha'i.

The slave murmured something, and Seshta realized that she had tensed, almost rising off the table. She forced herself to relax. She wouldn't leave Prince Penno's house until she learned something. She would speak to Miw's father, if nothing else. Maybe when Seshta told him what she knew, he would arrest the prince and torture him into telling where Reya was.

But she had nothing beyond her own suspicions. Reya's disappearance, after his melodramatic hints. Rumors about Meryey. The Libu's friendship with General Kha'i and now with Prince Penno. A vague overheard conversation. Frightening dreams.

She had nothing at all to convince the Eyes and Ears of Pharaoh that he should torture a prince. She needed more information.

Finally the slave helped Seshta dress in a lovely pleated gown. Seshta wondered if the prince had daughters or wives. She shrugged off the question and fidgeted while the woman applied her kohl and finally placed her wig—freshly cleaned—on her head. At last the slave stood back and studied Seshta.

Seshta smiled. "Yes, you've done a lovely job. Thank you." She started for the door.

The slave hurried beside her.

Seshta shook her head and put a hand on the woman's shoulder. "No, I can find my way." Seshta gave her a gentle push back into the room. "Stay here, please." The slave's forehead puckered, but she backed into the room and stopped.

Seshta hurried into the hallway. Now she could work! She could only vaguely remember which way they had come, but she didn't want the slave woman to come after her, so she plunged down the hall.

In just a few paces she reached a dead end, with doorways to left and right. A glance showed two bedrooms. Seshta hesitated. She should find Meryey and the prince and listen to their conversation. But how could she pass up the chance to search the prince's bedroom?

In the first room she spotted the end of a painted wooden cosmetic box under the bed. Probably a woman's room, then. Seshta turned to the other. Besides the wooden bed, the room held a carved ebony chair, baskets for linen storage, and three small wooden chests.

Seshta glanced back the way she'd come; the hall lay empty. She scuttled into the room and crouched in front of a chest. Perhaps Prince Penno kept papers of some kind in here. Seshta could read only a little, but she could smuggle the papers out and find a way to translate them.

Movement in the corner caught Seshta's eye and she gasped.

She shook her head and chuckled as a cat strolled over and rubbed against her leg. Seshta scratched its head, her heart still racing, and tried to believe she was not scared.

"I must hurry, little goddess," she whispered. "Which box first? This one?"

The cat mewed. Seshta opened the first chest and gazed down at a dozen sandals, neatly stacked. She grunted, closed the lid, and turned to the next box, a small chest inlaid with blue faience and pink-stained ivory. Surely such a precious box would hold something important! She pried up the lid.

Seshta stared at a lovely array of silver bracelets inlaid with precious stones. Well, she had one more box to search, and then she could try the baskets. Prince Penno might hide his papers under his clothing or in scroll cases under the bed. Of course, he might also have an office somewhere else in the compound, like her father did, or he might do all his work at a temple or government building.

"Are you lost, mistress?"

Seshta squealed and fell onto her backside.

A man stood in the doorway, dressed in the simple loincloth of a servant.

Seshta glanced at the open jewelry chest and felt her face burn. "I just—I only wondered—I—"

"Let me escort you to the garden, mistress."

Seshta closed the chest and stood. The man waited while she meekly stepped past him. She furiously tried to think through her humiliation. She had to keep the servant from telling Prince Penno that she had searched his room!

They walked through a sitting room to the central hall with its huge columns and stairs to the roof. What possible excuse could she give for looking at the prince's jewelry?

They passed through a small reception room. Maybe she could pretend she was looking for something harmless—something of her own.

They entered the vestibule that led to the garden. Seshta stopped and turned to the servant. "When I fell in the pond I lost a bracelet. I thought maybe someone had found it and thought it was the prince's. I didn't want to ask for it, because if it was really lost the prince might feel he had to replace it. But I thought if someone had found it and thought it was his, they might put it in his room, so I was just taking a look for it. That's all."

"Of course, mistress. I will ask if anyone has found your bracelet."

"Thank you. It's, um, turquoise—turquoise beads painted with Eyes of Horus."

"I am sure we will find it, mistress."

Seshta tried to smile brightly. She couldn't tell whether the man believed her or not; his face held no expression. He stepped toward an archway, where lamplight flickered from the garden beyond.

A voice floated through the doorway. "Where is she? It's been—"

The servant's voice drowned out the rest of the sentence. "Through this door, mistress. You will find all the others there."

"Thank you."

Seshta paused in the doorway, still trembling from nerves. Two men stood among some trees nearby, but she couldn't see who they were. Their voices drifted to her.

"What of the boy Reya?"

Seshta gasped.

"He is of no more use to us. Kill him in the morning."

Seshta swayed and grabbed for the doorframe. The voice of her heart pounded in her ears. She glanced back to see the servant walking away from her. No one was watching as she slid into the shadows near the garden door.

"He is safe enough for now?" Seshta thought she recognized the prince's voice.

"Quite safe." The second man had an accent. "He is locked in my stables, and it is impossible to lift the bar from inside."

"Is he well guarded?" the prince asked.

Seshta leaned forward and saw the other man in profile against the glow of distant torches. She recognized the Libu Meryey's curly beard and side braid. "Most of my men will be away from the house tonight," he said. "But there is a guard at the gate, and, of course, servants in the house."

"But no one at the stable door? Is that wise?"

"The boy cannot get out. Do not worry. In the morning they will find his body floating in the Nile."

Seshta pressed back against the wall and closed her eyes. A cold hand clamped around her heart. But if they thought no one would look for Reya, they were wrong. She knew what to do now. She would find Miw's father and make him get Reya out. She had proof now.

The Libu spoke again. "And what of the Eyes and Ears of Pharaoh, Lord Uben-Ra? Has he consented to join us?"

"Yes. I told you he could be bought. Come, let us rejoin the others before we're missed."

They walked toward the light and noise at the far end of the garden. Seshta slumped against the wall and tried to think through the haze in her mind. Reya was a prisoner at the Libu's house. Miw's father had joined the enemy.

She had to get to Reya that night. She had to save him herself, or he would die.

Chapter 18

Seshta felt like one of Horus's jointed wooden toys, hardly in control of her own body, as she stumbled through the garden.

She passed a grape arbor. Inside, the young Libu Ker bent his head close while Miw spoke, gesturing with her hands. Miw's glance flew to Seshta and her hands stilled. She touched Ker lightly on the arm and started toward Seshta.

Seshta turned and kept walking. Miw drew up beside her.

"Seshta, is everything all right?"

Seshta stopped walking but stared straight ahead. "Where's your father?"

"He was called away. Do you need him?"

Seshta clenched her hands to keep them from trembling. "No. I don't need him."

"Seshta, if you need help, ask for it." Miw grabbed Seshta's shoulder and moved in front of her. "Look, I know something is going on. I might even know what it is. But there isn't much time. Pharaoh is coming tomorrow morning!"

Seshta's head throbbed. What did Pharaoh have to do with this? Let him come and have his processional; that wouldn't save Reya.

Miw shook her. "If you know something, you have to tell me!"

"Miw? How do you know whom to trust?"

Miw stared back, then half-smiled and shrugged. "Sometimes you just have to trust."

Seshta studied her face. Miw wouldn't hurt or betray anyone. But how could she tell Miw that her father was a traitor? Miw would never believe that, and she'd go to him for help the moment Seshta said anything. Seshta glanced at the grape arbor. Ker stood in the shadows watching them.

"I'm sorry. There's nothing I can tell you." Seshta walked on and didn't look back.

She couldn't see Horus in the crowd at the far end of the garden. Some of the other girls called to her, wanting to gossip, but Seshta pushed past them. Prince Penno sat on a gilt chair near the pond, torchlight flickering on the gold at his chest and wrists. Seshta scanned the crowd around him. Meryey met her eyes and smiled.

She stumbled away, into the shadows.

"Seshta?"

She peered into the darkness and saw Horus in the corner.

She ran to him and grabbed his arms. "Horus!"

"Are you all right? You weren't hurt?"

"No, but—oh!" Her throat closed up and she couldn't speak.

Horus started talking softly. "I didn't find out much. Prince Penno knows General Kha'i, but he knows everyone in power. Meryey is here regularly; the prince buys his horses. The servants seemed surprised that Meryey is here tonight. They thought maybe the prince has a big purchase in mind and hopes to get a better deal by entertaining him. Nobody has heard anything about a young soldier."

He paused and peered into her face. "Are you all right now? Can you tell me what happened?"

"Prince Penno and Meryey—I hid in the bushes and heard everything."

"Good for you! What did they say?"

Seshta's voice trembled. "He plans to kill Reya in the morning."

Horus sucked in his breath. "You're sure? They actually said that?"

"The prince said, 'He is of no more use to us. Kill him in the morning,' and Meryey said he would. Horus, we have to get him out tonight."

"We need help. We have to tell someone now."

"We can't." Seshta glanced back. The light and laughter of the party seemed far away. "Miw's father has joined them."

Horus gasped. "The Eyes and Ears of Pharaoh? I don't believe it!"

"They bribed him. And if he can be bribed, anyone might be corrupt."

Horus sagged against the wall. "Has the whole world gone mad? What can we do?"

"We must free Reya ourselves. Meryey said there's only a guard at the gate tonight. The stables should be along the outer wall. If we can get over the wall, we can find Reya."

"Seshta... there is great evil at work here. More than we can handle alone."

"I know. But we can free Reya—I'm sure we can. He'll know what to do next. Once he's safe, we can tell everyone what happened and let them figure it out. But we have to save him first."

Horus clutched the amulet around his neck. "We should hire a priest to offer sacrifices before we attemp such a thing."

"We don't have time. We must do this tonight!"

"Now?"

Seshta hesitated. "If we disappear from the party, the priestess will notice and search for me. She'll tell Prince Penno."

Horus took a few steps and looked out at the people chatting, nibbling on food, or playing board games. "She can't plan to stay much longer. You have that contest in the morning."

Seshta groaned and put her hands to her eyes. "The contest. How will we get Reya out and report what happened and still get to the contest in time? I'm already bruised and aching and now it looks like I won't get any sleep tonight."

Tears welled up in her eyes. She had wanted to win the contest more than anything.

Seshta stood tall and took two deep breaths to calm herself. Her heart told her what she had to do. "It doesn't matter. There may be other contests. There's only one Reya."

"Tell the priestess you want to go home. I'll meet you outside the temple."

"All right. Give me an hour. Wait by the butcher stall. We will rescue Reya!"

Seshta found herself beside Sit-Hathor as the slaves carried the litters through the dark streets. Sit-Hathor cleared her throat. "I want to apologize again. I have behaved foolishly over this contest." She paused. "I suppose you know that I asked some of the others to spy on you?"

"Yes." Seshta could hardly believed she'd once cared.

"I'm sorry about that too. This contest is very important to me, and I went too far. I didn't realize how far until Idut.... It won't happen again. I really do want to win this contest on my merits, and I will see that everyone leaves you alone now. I hope you will forgive me."

Seshta sighed. At least she wouldn't have to worry about being followed when she went to rescue Reya. She and Horus could work unobserved.

She imagined sneaking through dark streets, trying to enter Meryey's house, facing unknown dangers. She trembled.

Sit-Hathor squirmed. "Well? Will you forgive me?"

An idea formed in Seshta's mind. "No."

"What!"

"I'm sorry, I didn't mean that. I'll forgive you, but I want you to do something for me."

Sit-Hathor hesitated, took a breath, and said, "Anything."

"Tell the other girls you still want to know what I'm doing. Tell them... tell them you think I'm going to find a magic spell tonight to help me win. Offer a big reward if they watch me closely and follow everyplace I go."

"In Hathor's name, why?"

"And don't ask why."

Sit-Hathor studied her through narrowed eyes. Finally she said, "I don't understand, but all right. You ask for this favor, and I will grant it, to make amends."

She shook her head. "I just hope this ends the way you wish."

Seshta looked out at the night. "So do I."

Chapter 19

Seshta left Sit-Hathor whispering to some other girls and hurried to her room. She changed into a coarsely woven tan dress and then said a prayer to steady herself. Her heart raced as if she'd just run across the whole city.

She stepped her feet close together and stretched her arms up high, lengthening her spine. Then she bent forward at the waist, laying her chest against her thighs and her forehead to her shins. As she took slow, deep breaths, her muscles released their tension.

When she felt calmer, she straightened and peered into the hallway. Other doors stood partly open, and faces peeked out through the cracks. Seshta hid a smile. These girls could never follow her if she wanted to get away unseen. None except Miw....

She wouldn't think of Miw. Miw might figure out what Seshta was really doing, but she wouldn't have time to tell her father until Reya was out and safe. Then it wouldn't matter who knew.

Seshta slipped along the hallway, ignoring the murmur and shuffle behind her. She checked that nothing moved in the courtyard. She had to get her followers out of the temple complex unseen as well as herself. If the girls got caught, Seshta could still escape alone, but she didn't want that. She wanted witnesses.

Guards watched the main gate, so Seshta led the way past the kitchens and stables to the rear of the complex. She crept up the steps of one of the beehive-shaped granaries. She paused, studied the distance to the outer wall, and leaped. She landed in a crouch on the wall and steadied herself. Seshta didn't look back toward the whispering at the granary. She just hoped the other girls could follow her.

The alley below lay empty. As she walked along the wall, she imagined the girls strung out in a line behind her, like ducklings behind their mother. She would have laughed if fear for Reya hadn't filled her heart.

She reached the corner and had to turn before lowering herself. Two girls stood behind her on the wall. The first backed up and bumped the other; they grabbed at each other, swaying. Seshta held her breath until the girls caught their balance. Then she lowered her eyes and pretended not to see them huddling as if they could hide behind each other.

Another girl stood on top of the granary, ready to jump, and Seshta caught a glimpse of someone still on the steps. She didn't see Miw.

Seshta lowered herself to the soft mound of a garbage pile and wrinkled her nose as her feet sank into the stinky muck. She picked her way down the pile and tried not to breathe until she got several paces away.

She paused at the end of the alley, pretending to study the street as she waited for the others to catch up. She heard a grunt followed by swearing and wondered with a smile which of the girls had lost her footing in the trash.

Seshta waited while a couple of drunken sailors staggered down the street, and then she hurried toward the butcher's stall. Horus pulled her into the shadows beside it.

"Someone's following you!" he whispered.

Seshta glanced back at the darting figures, so easy to spot in their pale dresses. "It's all right. They're some of the dancers. I want someone to know where we are."

"You told them?"

"No, they think it's something about the contest. I just wanted... well, if something goes wrong, I want people to know where we went."

Horus gulped. "If something goes wrong—"

"It won't. Don't worry."

"No. It's a good idea—the other girls."

"Come on then. You brought some rope? That was smart."

"I thought we might need it to get over the wall or something." He took a deep breath. "All right, let's go."

They scurried through the dusty streets in the moonlight. They passed a few other people, mostly men heading home from the taverns. Seshta's heart thudded when a night watchman nodded in greeting, but no one stopped them.

Soon they reached Meryey's estate. "This is it," Seshta whispered. "The gate is down that street, so we have to get in on this side."

The night air felt warm and still, but Seshta didn't think that was why Horus's forehead glistened with sweat. He put a fist to his stomach as if it pained him. "How do we get over the wall?"

Seshta stared up at the plastered bricks. "Give me a boost. If I stand on your shoulders, I think I can reach the top."

"What about me? You can't pull me up."

"No... you wait here."

Horus hesitated. "No. You might need me." He shrugged and tried to smile. "Besides, I'll worry too much if I don't know what's going on. I'll boost you up and then hand up the rope. Tie it to something and drop down the end."

"Good idea. We can leave it here for a fast escape."

He crouched. Seshta climbed onto his shoulders. Horus stood slowly while they both pressed their hands against the wall for balance.

Seshta peered over the wall. Only it wasn't a wall, it was a flat roof, stretching several paces in front of her and extending the entire length of the estate. She glanced around and her heart skipped a beat. A dozen figures lay on the roof a few paces away. Servants, sleeping up where the air was cooler.

They didn't stir. Finally, Seshta breathed again. She squinted at the dark estate, trying to pick out buildings. The two-story structure ahead must be the house. If the servants' quarters were to her right, beneath the sleeping figures, then this long building probably held the kitchens and horse stables as well. Reya might be right underneath her!

She heard a muffled grunt from below and remembered Horus. Seshta hauled herself onto the roof, watching the servants for signs of wakefulness. She leaned down to take the rope from Horus's outstretched hand and pointed toward the corner of the roof away from the sleeping servants. Horus trotted alongside the wall while Seshta tiptoed across the roof.

The corner of the roof held a small raised platform, purely decorative, but high enough that she could tie the rope around it. She let one end dangle down to Horus and motioned him up.

Horus grabbed the rope, put a foot against the wall, and began to haul himself up. His breathing sounded loud. Seshta glanced around to make sure no one noticed them. The servants slept on. The street appeared empty. Where were the temple girls? Had they gotten lost somewhere in the city?

Horus scrambled over the edge of the roof and knelt beside her. He gasped at the servants and grabbed his amulet. "By the god's eye—"

"Shh, they're sleeping. Let's hurry."

Seshta led the way across the roof toward the courtyard. She looked over the edge at a large oval horse trough full of water. Seshta lowered herself to the trough's wide edge and then dropped to the ground. Horus followed.

They stood close together in a corner of Meryey's estate. Seshta felt all her senses straining to penetrate the night. She heard the murmur of a faint breeze stirring the trees, and then a rustling, perhaps mice scrabbling for spilled grain. In the distance a dog barked and another answered. Seshta shivered as she realized how lucky they were that Meryey didn't have dogs on guard.

She took two steps and put her hand on the nearest door. It swung open at her touch. She stared at the shapes huddled in the darkness. "Reya?" she whispered, though she knew the door to his prison would be barred. As her eyes adjusted to the light, she identified chariot wheels, an axle, and harnesses hanging from the wall.

Seshta let out her breath and pulled the door shut. She grabbed Horus's hand. His palm was clammy but his grip strong as she led him around the horse trough to the next door. They'd seen the tack room, so the stable was close. Reya had to be near.

Small, dark windows pierced the wall. The smell of horses and straw told Seshta this must be the stable. Her heart thrummed in her chest, telling her that Reya was close, so close!

A huge wooden bar ran across the door and nestled in a slot in the wall—no normal stable door, but surely one meant to trap more than horses.

Seshta's skin tingled with awareness the way it did just before an important dance. She looked at Horus, his expression hidden in the shadows. Together they lifted the bar.

The door creaked open. A hoof clomped against the floor. A horse snorted.

Seshta and Horus stood in the doorway, staring into the gloom. A solid wall stood on their right, while to the left a horse gazed over a half wall. Beyond that horse, more animals stood in a series of stalls separated by low walls.

In front of them, in the corner, Seshta saw a dark lump, like a pile of blankets.

The lump moved.

Seshta gasped and clutched Horus's hand. The horse whinnied faintly. The lump sat up.

"Reya?"

"Who...?" His voice cracked. "It can't be!"

She flew to him. He flinched at her touch, but then returned her embrace.

She loosened her hold and knelt beside him. "You're hurt!"

"Never mind. You have to get out of here—you shouldn't have come!"

"We'll all get out, right now."

Reya pushed against the wall and struggled to his feet. He moved stiffly, like an old man, and his voice rasped in his throat. "How did you get past the guards?"

Seshta took his arm. "There aren't any tonight, except at the gate."

Horus yelped.

"Shush!" Seshta looked at Horus and froze. He was backing towards them.

Two men stood in the doorway, silhouetted by moonlight.

Chapter 20

Nobody moved.

Seshta tried to think of something to say. If these men were only servants and didn't know why Reya was here, maybe they could bluff their way out. Her mind churned, but when she opened her mouth, nothing came out.

The two men stepped through the doorway. They had the hair and tattoos of the Libu. They carried swords.

One of them said, "Meryey was right. Egyptians really are foolish enough to walk into a simple trap."

Reya pushed in front of Seshta. "They don't know anything, I swear."

The man smiled. "I believe that. A pity, since we went to so much trouble to watch them after their visit to the barracks. But this is too important to let a couple of flies ruin it by buzzing too loudly."

Seshta tried to make sense of his words through the haze of fear. "You mean you knew all along? Meryey knew I was listening to him at the party?"

"He made sure you would." The man laughed. "You shouldn't challenge a master if you don't know how to play the game."

Reya spread his arms as if he could hold back their enemies. "Please...."

"You won't be stupid enough to ask me to let them go," the man said. "You know better. Meryey will decide how to deal with you all when he gets back. But now we have real work to do."

Reya looked back at Seshta. In the moonlight coming in through the door, she could see dark bruises on his face. Horus pressed against the wall, the whites of his eyes huge.

Seshta fumbled for Reya's hand. He returned her grip and stood straighter, staring at the Libu. Horus edged closer and the three stood shoulder to shoulder.

The man who had spoken chuckled. He turned and marched away. The other guard followed him and pulled the door shut.

The bar scraped against the wood as it settled into place. They stood in darkness and silence.

Seshta ran to the door and pushed, although she knew it wouldn't open. The voice of her heart pounded in her ears, louder than a drum. What a fool she'd been.

She leaned her forehead against the door and closed her eyes. They would find a way out. They had to. She ran her hands over the coarse wooden planks, too thick to break. She felt the cold metal hinges riveted deep into the wood.

They weren't getting through this door.

"Oh, Amun!" Reya moaned. "I'm so sorry you got into this. If I'd known...."

"You couldn't have stopped us." Seshta turned to the dim forms of Horus and Reya in the darkness. "We wanted to find you, and we did. But they were watching us."

"It's my fault," Reya said. "At first, I said I'd already told other people, but I refused to give names. I thought they'd keep me alive if I had information they wanted. Later... later they did things to get me to talk." His voice dropped. "I would have told them anything then. I'm not proud of it, but it's true."

Seshta winced. She wanted to comfort him, but something about his hunched shoulders and bowed head, beaten and humiliated, held her back.

Horus said, "I would have told too. I guess it doesn't help, but I know I would have."

Seshta said, "But you didn't tell us anything important! So when you told them the truth—"

"They didn't believe me. Can you imagine? When I finally told the truth, they didn't believe me. The General insisted I'd told someone. That's why they noticed you, I guess."

"But what's going on?" Horus asked. "Reya, what did he mean about how important this is?"

Reya leaned against the wall with a sigh. "It means I was a fool. I overheard some men talking about their plan, but I got it wrong."

"Tell us," Seshta said. She wanted to scream and kick and throw herself against their prison walls, but she also wanted to understand. The Libu had called this a game. They had to understand the game if they hoped to win.

"It's a plot to kill Pharaoh. There's a whole company of Libu in our army, prisoners of war and mercenaries, two hundred men with their own commander. They don't all know about this, but when their general commands them, they will do what he says. Some royals are involved too, and an Egyptian general."

"General Kha'i."

"No, that was my mistake. I thought he was the one, so I went to General Menna." Reya sighed.

"What happened?" Horus asked.

"Menna is the traitor. Menna and Meryey, and a prince, I don't know which one."

"Prince Penno," Seshta said. "At least we found out that."

"Oh, that's helpful," Reya said. "We could tell someone if we could get out of here."

"We will get out," Seshta said. "We must!"

Reya snorted. "Don't you think I've tried?"

Seshta hated the bitterness and despair in his voice. What had happened in the last few days to change him so much?

She remembered his bruises and felt queasy. Maybe she would rather not know. "Have you been here the whole time? In these stables, I mean."

"No. They had me somewhere else—a storeroom—until this evening. I wondered why they moved me. Now I know. They wanted to make it easier for you to find me."

"Have you tried—I mean really tried—to get out of this room?"

"The door is barred and the windows are too small."

"Let me try the window, I'm smaller than you." Seshta slipped past the horse in the closest stall. Her heart sank as she neared the window opening. It was barely as big as her head.

She stood on her toes and thrust her head through the window. The mud brick of the window edge brushed against her chin and the top of her head. The yard seemed bright after the shadows of the stables. Moonlight poured silver onto the hard-packed dirt, and the scent of jasmine drifted past like perfume.

She glanced to the side. Someone stood a few paces away.

Seshta jerked back and scraped her head on the top of the window. She grunted and stumbled in the straw. The horse backed away, snorting at her.

Seshta brushed off her dress as she squeezed past the horse and out of the stall. "It's no good. I can't get through, and a guard is watching the door."

"They can't really mean to kill Pharaoh," Horus said. "How? And... and why?"

Reya sank to the floor. His voice sounded hoarse and weary. "For power, of course. During his visit here, Pharaoh will be away from the bulk of the army, and the Libu can escape north quickly. By the time the news reaches the capital, it will all be over. General Menna and your prince will chase the Libu out of the city and return looking like heroes for routing the enemy."

"But what good will that do them?" Seshta asked. "There are other ways to look like a hero."

"This prince must be in line for the throne somewhere," Reya said. "He must hope to seize power in the confusion after Pharaoh dies, and this will make him look strong and important."

"He is in line," Seshta said, "but not one of the first."

Reya shrugged. "No doubt others will challenge him, but Pharaoh's sons are all young, and a few bribes and favors exchanged with the priests and royal court can buy a lot of backing. Or even arrange for an 'illness' to sweep through the royal nursery."

Seshta shuddered. "And Meryey is just in it for the money?"

Reya frowned. "Hard to say. He's definitely getting money, but he also seems to hate and resent Egypt. He may think this will weaken the country so much that the Libu can attack. His heart is evil, but it's also clever. He may be using the prince."

Seshta shivered and hugged herself. "So how much time do we have? When does this all happen?"

"They'll attack Pharaoh during his processional, whenever that is. I've lost track of time."

"In the morning," Seshta said. "In just a few hours!"

They stared at each other. Reya said slowly, "Then that's when it will happen. They're going to kill Pharaoh today."

They were silent, awed by the very idea of trying to kill the Living God.

Finally Seshta said, "So that's what Miw meant. She said something about Pharaoh, but I didn't understand. I was just worried about you, Reya. I didn't see."

"The other girls," Horus said. "They're still out there, right?"

Reya stirred in the darkness. "What are you talking about?"

"Some of the temple dancers," Seshta said. "I got them to follow us. They don't know about you; they think we're doing something else. But they should be out there, somewhere, if they didn't get lost. But I don't know what they'll do. If we don't come out, they might just give up and go home. They might not say anything until tomorrow, when I don't show up for the contest. And then everyone will be too busy, and it will be too late."

"We're right next to the street," Horus said. "We could yell for help."

Reya jerked as if he'd been stabbed. "No. The guards will hear, and they'll come for you."

Seshta cringed. "Anyway, the girls might try to get in or ask about us at the gate."

"We can't do that to them," Horus croaked.

"No. In the morning, with crowds outside, we might try it. We might have to. But not yet." Seshta paced. "I only saw one guard outside. They must not think we're too much of a threat."

"They know I'm not," Reya muttered.

"Stop it!" Seshta said. "Why are you so hard on yourself? You made one mistake, and you got caught by people older and nastier and more experienced than you. What were you supposed to do then, when you were locked up and guarded day and night?"

She crossed the floor and dropped to her knees in front of him. Horus crouched beside her. Reya sat cross-legged, his shoulders slumped and his head bowed. Seshta could hardly hear him when he spoke. "It was a pretty big mistake."

"Don't you think I feel stupid, too?" she said. "This whole time, I thought I was spying on them, and it was the other way around. They made a complete fool of me."

"You're not a soldier."

"And you've only been one for a year! You're still in training; you've never even been in battle."

"And now I never will be."

Seshta bit back her irritation. "What I mean is, you have plenty of time to become a great warrior. Nobody expects it of you when you're sixteen."

She reached for his arm. "Are the other new recruits all so wonderful? Why didn't they discover Meryey's plot? Why didn't your superiors? Maybe you didn't save Egypt single-handed, but you tried. And you're much better than people like General Menna and Prince Penno. They're traitors."

Reya gazed at her, but she couldn't read his expression in the dim light. "I know."

He sighed. "I know all of that, I guess, but still... they're going to kill Pharaoh, and I couldn't stop them. And now you're in danger, too, that's the worst thing I could have done. If it were just about me, I wouldn't mind so much, but Seshta, *they're going to kill the Living God!* Maybe I didn't betray Pharaoh, but I failed him."

Seshta stiffened her shoulders. "Not yet. We still have a few hours. We must find a way to escape and warn Pharaoh."

Chapter 21

"What if we yell for the guard," Seshta said, "and pretend one of us is sick or something. If we can get him to open the door—"

"It won't work."

"Reya, we haven't even tried it!"

"I did try it. When I first got here."

"Oh. They didn't open the door?"

"They opened it," Reya said. "And I was standing there ready to smash someone in the head with a clay pot. But the guard had called for help first, and the door opened with three of them side by side, holding swords."

"Oh."

"And then they beat me to teach me a lesson."

"Reya, I'm sorry... I didn't know."

He sighed. "It doesn't matter now. But I don't want them to hurt you too."

"What about the horses?" Horus said. "Could we get one to kick down the door?"

"We'd probably just hurt ourselves," Seshta said. "One of my father's horses saw a snake and panicked; he nearly killed the man leading him before they got him under control. Anyway, the door is thick. It would take time and make a lot of noise, and they'd be waiting when we got out."

Reya crossed to the door and slammed his palm against it. "It's hopeless. Anything we can come up with, they've already thought of and made sure it won't work."

"But maybe they're counting on that attitude!" Seshta said. "Meryey thinks you won't fight back anymore, and Horus and I are young, and I'm a girl.

He won't see us as a threat, especially after he tricked us so easily. Maybe he got careless. He didn't even tie us up or move us back to your storeroom."

Reya leaned against the door, mouth half open.

Horus said, "I don't have much courage or a clever heart. I didn't know if we could ever find you, and I've been afraid this whole time. But I followed Seshta because we cared about you and we wanted to do anything we could to help you, because it was right. Because you're worth it." He shrugged. "Anyway, I'd rather try to get out than wait to see what they do to us in the morning."

Reya stared as if he'd never seen them before. Seshta almost smiled. They had known each other forever, and they could still surprise each other.

Horus knelt by the wall on the street side and pulled out the knife he used for carving wood. He started chipping at the mud bricks, leaving thin white scratches. No one said what they all knew, that it would take far too long to break through to the street. Meryey might return at any moment, but even if he didn't, they wouldn't get through the wall before morning.

Finally Reya said, "The ceiling might be easier to get through than the wall."

Horus stood. "Yes, of course. It's just mud poured over thatch. It might be looser."

They gazed up at the rough ceiling. A grid of wooden beams supported a mixture of mud and straw.

Reya climbed up on the half wall that formed the horse's stall. "Give me your knife." Horus passed it to him. Reya raised the knife and stabbed at the mud over his head. Seshta's arms ached just watching him reach up like that.

Horus touched her elbow. "Let me have your sash." He slipped into the horse stall and dipped the sash into the small water trough. He climbed up beside Reya to press the wet cloth against the mud. "Maybe it will help soften the brick." Trickles of mud ran down his arm.

Seshta searched the stalls where three horses and a donkey dozed. A couple of leather harnesses hung from pegs on the wall, and the stalls each had a small stone water trough. Other than that, and the musty hay and horse dung, the thick walls and hard-packed dirt floor were bare. She tried every window, but they were all too small, and all led into the courtyard where the guard stood.

Horus said, "If we had a way to start a fire, we could light the straw on fire and try to burn through the ceiling."

Reya grunted. "Then I'm glad we don't have a fire. Granted, we would attract attention—what with flames, screaming horses, and falling rubble—but I'm not sure we'd survive to explain."

"It was just a thought."

Reya smiled at him. Seshta gazed up at them, so different from each other and from her, but her best friends in the world. Whatever happened that night, or in the morning, she could face better with them. She closed her eyes and said a prayer to the Goddess that they might be brave and clever enough to find a way through this maze of evil.

Time passed, feeling like eternity. Seshta paced the narrow corridor along the stalls. Mice rustled in the hay, and Seshta saw a rat skulking along the wall. She scratched insect bites, coughed in the dust, and wondered about the other girls. Surely they had all gone back to the temple by now, to sleep before their big day, the event of a lifetime, performing for Pharaoh.

Seshta's moment of envy faded. If no one warned Pharaoh, this day would be memorable indeed, but not in a way any of them wanted.

Horus now had the knife and Reya held the muddy sash. Seshta could see the fatigue in their trembling arms as they reached for the ceiling. They had not yet pierced the roof.

The window seemed lighter already, the first gray before dawn. It was almost time for morning prayers, which would set the day into the proper alignment as Ra drove his fiery chariot across the sky.

Would Meryey return to deal with them now, or was he too busy with his other plans? The dance contest would start soon, and Pharaoh's processional would follow.

She heard muffled sounds from across the estate. A cat yowled, like a call for help. The world outside was waking up, and no one knew that Pharaoh was in danger.

Except Miw. She had known something was wrong. And her father was not, after all, a traitor. Prince Penno had told that lie knowing Seshta was listening.

Could Miw be out in the street, wondering what had happened to them? If only Seshta could get a message to her.

Maybe she could. She did a handstand and paced the floor on her hands while she thought.

"Practicing?" Reya said. "What dedication. Or are you bored? I'm sorry if we're not entertaining enough."

Seshta dropped to her feet. "Reya, what do you think the guards would do if I started singing?"

Chapter 22

"It's almost dawn," Seshta said. "Would they let me sing my morning prayer? Maybe I can send a message to the girls, if anyone is listening."

Reya wiped at his forehead, leaving a streak of mud. "We can try."

Seshta stood by the door and put her mouth near the gap where the door didn't quite meet the wall. She hoped her voice would carry outside. Reya jumped down from the wall and stood near her.

Seshta tried to calm her fluttering heart. She closed her eyes, breathed deeply, and imagined herself in the temple courtyard with the other girls beside her and the priestess leading them. Her voice croaked at first, but got stronger as she sang the familiar lines.

Amun Re rises in the east
His rays lighten the land
And give life to the people of Egypt
Oh, Amun, give Pharaoh health, life, and old age
A long reign and strength in his limbs.

THUMP, THUMP!
Seshta jumped as the guard pounded on the door inches from her face. "What you do?" he growled. "You make quiet!"

Reya squeezed Seshta's shoulder and called out, "She's a priestess of the goddess Hathor! She has to pray. You wouldn't keep her from her religious duty, would you?"

Seshta told herself to keep singing, no matter what, but she felt like a demon was squeezing her chest.

The guard grunted in another language, but the door didn't open.

Reya whispered, "Go on!"

Seshta squeezed her eyes shut and tried to think of words that would sound like the prayer but would carry a message.

Oh, Amun, protect Pharaoh from His enemies
Pharaoh has many enemies
They are in the city, in the streets,

THUMP, THUMP! "Quiet I say! I call Meryey!" The door rattled.

Seshta rushed on, calling louder, her voice fast and shrill.

They are in His army, in His family
They will come when He least expects it
When His heart is filled with Holy thoughts
When the temple maidens dance in the streets
The Living God is not safe
Oh, Amun, protect Him from the general with an evil heart
Protect Him from the brother who would take His place.

She dared not give their names. If Miw was listening, she would hear the changes and understand what Seshta meant.

Seshta opened her eyes and stared at her friends. Horus turned from a courtyard window and grinned. "It's all right. He looks angry, but he isn't going for help or anything."

"Thank Amun," Reya whispered. "He didn't understand. Or else everybody is too busy to be interrupted. By now, they must be getting ready to go—" He broke off and shook his head. "Great performance." He patted Seshta's shoulder.

"If only someone heard me! We haven't much time."

"Should we keep working on the ceiling?" Horus asked. "Just in case?"

Reya glanced at the pale window. "We'll never get—" He stopped and gave them a stiff smile. "Yes, just in case. I *think* I can still lift my arms." He climbed onto the half wall with a groan.

Seshta leaned her forehead on the doorjamb and waited for her trembling to stop. Was Miw out there? Would she act in time? Already the first edge of dawn brightened the courtyard outside and a bird chirped. She stared through the crack between door and doorframe. A crack as thin as a knife's blade. If only she could slip through like a wisp of smoke.

She closed her eyes and imagined her *ba* flying free of her body, through the crack and out into the air. But so long as that wooden bar crossed the door, her body was trapped. She looked down at the thin strip of the bar visible through the crack, just a finger-length away. Outside, they could lift it easily. But from in here—

"Wait." The boys turned toward her. "Look at this! The door doesn't fit tight. There's a gap, and I can see the bar on the other side."

She backed away to give them room to look. She was afraid to say what she was thinking, afraid that it wouldn't work and the hope burning in her heart would die. "If we can stick the knife through and lift up the bar... if we could move it...."

She counted the beats of her heart as she waited for their answer.

"It might work," Reya said. "It might."

"If the knife is long enough," Horus said. "If we can get enough leverage. The bar will be heavy. And there's still the guard."

Reya turned and paced. "But only one guard." He stopped and straightened his shoulders. "I can distract the guard while you two get away. I only need to hold him for a few moments until you're over the wall."

"No," Seshta whispered. "He'll kill you."

"I'll have the knife."

They gazed at the knife, now dulled and chipped, its tip broken off. But the knife's quality didn't matter, because the guard's sword would cut down Reya before he ever got close enough to use it. They had done all this to save Reya, and he would die.

Reya put an arm around her. "It's the only way, my princess. You have to warn Pharaoh. That's all that matters now."

"What if you had a sling?" Horus gestured toward one of the harnesses hanging from a peg. "I can make a sling from that; it won't take long. You just need something to put in it to throw."

Reya gave a gusty sigh of relief. "Brilliant!" He slapped Horus on the back. "Your clever hands may save me yet."

Seshta blinked away her tears. A sling couldn't match a sword, but at least it gave Reya a chance.

Horus grabbed the harness, sat down cross-legged, and began working. Reya slid the knife through the gap between the door and doorframe. Seshta crouched beside him as he pressed the back of the knife blade up against the bar on the other side.

Reya grunted. "The knife's not quite long enough. I can touch the bar, but I don't know if I can move it."

"Oh, please, you have to!" Seshta said.

"Here." Horus held out the harness. "I don't need the whole thing. Cut the strap here, and take the rest.

See if you can get it through the crack and loop it around the bar. Then you can pull up with the strap."

Seshta gazed at Horus as Reya sawed through the leather. She had always believed Horus wasn't clever. Good with his hands, yes, but that was different. She had never before appreciated the cleverness that guided those hands. As she and Reya turned back to the door, their eyes met. Reya raised his eyebrows and smiled. Seshta knew he was thinking the same thing.

"Look out the window," Reya told Seshta. "Make sure the guard doesn't notice us."

She slipped into the first stall, stood on her toes, and peered out the window. Now she could see the courtyard clearly under a sky the washed-out pale blue of dawn. The Sun God must be nearing the horizon in his chariot. *Please,* Seshta thought, *don't hurry! Just take a little longer. For Pharaoh.*

The guard leaned against a wall eating a piece of flatbread. Seshta turned away from the window and hissed, "He's across the courtyard, ten paces away. He looks bored."

"Good," Reya grunted.

Getting the leather strip out and over the bar was easy enough. Getting it underneath the bar and back to them seemed impossible. The end bobbed outside the door and refused to be drawn back in.

Reya swore as he tried, for the hundredth time, to guide the leather in with the knife point. Seshta kept glancing from the guard to Reya.

Horus stood up. He had woven straw into a diamond shape, as big as his palm, to hold a stone. Long strips of leather extended a forearm's length on either side of the straw. "I wove the straw right around the leather strap," Horus said. "It will fall apart with use, but we only need it for a moment. Now we just need something to throw."

"What about that bit of ceiling you pulled down?"

Horus found the chunk, but it crumbled in his hands. "It got too wet. It's falling apart."

They searched the stable for a loose stone but didn't find one. Seshta wiped sweat from her forehead and sneezed in the dust they raised. "There's nothing here except straw and—" She giggled. Her whole body was tight with fear, so why did she feel giddy and reckless, like she might burst into hysterical laughter at any moment? "Um, Reya? How do you feel about flinging horse dung at the guard?"

He snorted a laugh. "Well, it won't kill him, but it might slow him down." He shook his head. "If the troops could see me now. I got the strap around the bar. If you're ready, we'll see if this works."

Chapter 23

Reya nestled a piece of the dung into the sling. He held two more chunks in his left hand. "I'll need some space to swing this. Get the door open and run. Don't wait for me. Don't even look back. Get out of here and warn Pharaoh; we don't have much time."

Seshta gazed at Reya. He was filthy and bruised, with stubble shading his scalp and chin. She remembered how he had looked that day at the riverside, laughing and handsome. Now, standing in the dim, dusty stable, he looked too small, fragile, no longer a heroic idol.

She felt a great rush of love and threw her arms around him. "Take care."

His body relaxed and he returned her hug with one arm. Seshta took a quick, shaky breath and joined Horus by the door. She hiked up her dress and knotted it at her hip so she could run without hindrance.

Horus grabbed the leather strip that looped around the door's bar. He pulled up until it went taut.

Nothing else moved. Seshta heard a chariot in the distance, her heart beating, and the buzz of a fly.

Horus tugged, jostling the door to wiggle the bar loose. "It's coming," he whispered.

Creaaak!

Horus pushed on the door. "Oof. Not quite."

"Hurry," Seshta hissed. "The guard must have heard that."

Horus yanked on the leather straps and rammed his shoulder against the door. The wood shook and rattled.

Horus's hands jerked up as the bar came free. He threw himself against the door and heaved it open, stumbling from the force of his push. Seshta ran out and grabbed his arm to steady him.

The guard ran toward them, drawing his sword.

"Out of the way!" Reya yelled.

Seshta pulled Horus to the left. In a few steps they reached the water trough where they had climbed down earlier. Seshta put her hand on the edge and looked back.

The guard was only two paces from Reya. His curved sword gleamed in the early light.

Reya's arm swung through the air. The dung flew from the sling and hit the guard's face.

The guard grunted and staggered back, shaking his head and snorting.

With one smooth movement, Reya loaded another piece of dung and let it fly. It hit the guard's throat. He made a gagging sound and grabbed his neck.

Reya ran toward Seshta. "Go!"

She scrambled onto the trough. Horus reached down and dragged her up to the roof. She looked back as Reya reached the wall. The guard darted behind him, sword raised for a strike.

"Watch out!" Seshta screamed.

As the sword sliced the air, Reya turned and flung the last piece of dung. The guard ducked back and his sword jerked from its path, brushing past Reya's left arm.

Reya leaped onto the trough. Blood flowed from a gash on his shoulder. "Get out of here!"

He put both hands on the roof to haul himself up, but his injured arm collapsed beneath him. His foot slipped off the trough and he clung to the roof with his good arm, half-dangling.

The guard vaulted onto the horse trough and walked along its broad edge, grinning.

Seshta cried out. For a moment the world seemed to spin. Then it ground to a halt, everything deathly clear as Lord Ra rose and cast a sunbeam across the roof, directly into the guard's face. The man paused, squinting against the glare.

Seshta launched herself toward him in a leap worthy of any dance contest. Arms out for balance, right foot stretched ahead and left pointing behind, she flew through the air.

Her foot hit the guard in the chest. He grunted and staggered off the end of the trough. His sword spun glittering in the sunlight and splashed in the water.

Seshta tucked her feet underneath her and imagined herself landing with perfect grace. Her heart soared. She felt invincible.

Her feet touched the trough wall, but the force of her leap threw her forward. She struggled for balance.

Seshta gave a strangled scream as she pitched forward. Her hands scrabbled for a hold, her knee scraped brick.

She tumbled into the water trough.

Seshta scrambled up, gasping and spluttering. The world spun again, bright light shattering the air around her. Her head reeled, water blurred her vision, and a cough tore at her lungs. She shook water from her face and gazed up.

Reya, his face lit with laughter, stood on the trough and held his good arm down to her.

Seshta grabbed Reya's hand. He hauled her up and pushed her in front of him toward the roof. She staggered forward and grasped the roof's edge with shaking hands.

She looked past Horus's feet to the crowd of Meryey's servants. They no longer slept on the rooftop. They were up and coming toward her.

Horus pulled Seshta while Reya pushed from behind. She wanted to tell them that she could move faster on her own, but she didn't have time to speak. Anyway, her legs trembled, and she was glad to kneel for a moment on the roof's edge to help pull up Reya.

She turned and rose as Horus ran for the far side of the roof.

The first of the servants grabbed him.

Horus yelped and struggled. The servant let go and staggered back, clutching his side. Seshta had a vague impression of something sticking from the man's ribs, but she didn't waste time trying to understand. She dodged more servants. One grabbed her shoulder; she scratched at his wrist and jerked away. Another reached for her.

She choked on a sob. Meryey's people had them, they would never escape.

Horus reached the far edge of the roof and grabbed the rope. He slid down quickly with a grunt of pain.

Seshta ducked under an outstretched arm and stumbled after him. Her hands shook as she grabbed the rope. She turned and lowered her body over the edge.

Reya stood a pace away, his back to her, unarmed, even the empty sling lost in the confusion. Seshta saw the guard haul himself up on the other side of the roof. Other bodies moved in from the side.

Seshta's head dropped below the wall and the rope burned her hands. She hit the ground and collapsed.

Hands grabbed her, pulled her up, pushed her into the street. She'd been captured! She stumbled as someone dragged her across the street. Images blurred together, the air swirled with dust and noise. Shouts, the clanking of metal. People, too many people, men with weapons and shields. They had failed, Meryey had caught them, they were too late....

"Seshta!"

She blinked away tears and stared at the small figure holding her shoulders. "Miw?"

"Are you all right?"

Seshta's mouth opened and closed. Horus stood a pace away, staring back at Meryey's compound. Seshta turned and saw the street filled with soldiers— Egyptian soldiers in plain kilts, raising longbows or carrying spears and cowhide shields. Some knelt and boosted the others up to the roof. Meryey's servants scattered.

Reya still stood on the edge of the roof. The guard swung his sword. As the blade cut the air, Reya turned and jumped. The sword slashed harmlessly behind him as he dropped to the street.

Soldiers reached the roof. The guard turned and ran.

Seshta's legs buckled and Miw helped lower her to the ground. Seshta looked up to see Reya striding toward her, one arm drenched in blood. He grinned down and she smiled back. She couldn't speak.

Horus thumped Reya on his good shoulder. "That sling work was amazing!"

"Thanks. Hello, Miw. You got Seshta's message?"

"Yes. I've been here most of the night, waiting. I sent the other girls home. But it took some time to call the soldiers, and then we didn't want to attack until we knew where you were."

Miw smiled at Seshta. "When you started singing, I thanked the gods! I didn't know what you were doing, singing in a place like that, until I heard the changes you made!" She laughed.

"It helped, then?" Seshta said. "Miw, what about Pharaoh? We have to warn him, they'll attack any moment—"

"Don't worry, we're taking care of it. The soldiers are ready for them."

Miw got a linen bandage from someone and wrapped Reya's wound. Quiet settled over the street.

A few soldiers still paced in the dust, but most had moved into the compound. An occasional shout drifted back to them.

"You already knew, didn't you?" Seshta said. "All this—it was for nothing? You knew about the plot?"

"Most of it," Miw said. "You helped clear up some details. We weren't sure how involved Prince Penno was until last night."

"But I didn't even tell you what I heard."

"No, but I could tell you'd learned something. That was a clue. And we didn't know how Reya was involved, whose side he was really on." She winked at him. "General Kha'i has a few words for you."

Reya groaned. "I'll bet he does, and most of them curses. I can't believe I went to Menna and told him General Kha'i was behind all this."

"Don't worry about it now," Miw said. "The worst is over, and you're still alive. Does anything else really matter?"

Seshta gasped. "The contest! I guess I missed it."

Miw smiled. "We both did. But there are more important things than winning a contest, right?"

"I guess so." Seshta looked at Miw, at Horus, at Reya—dirty and bruised, but with the glint of mischief back in his eyes. "Maybe even some things more important than dancing."

Chapter 24

"We will all go to the palace," Miw said. "Pharaoh will want to hear how things ended."

Seshta, Reya, and Horus exchanged nervous glances. Would Pharaoh be pleased with their behavior or angry at their mistakes? It did not do to upset the Living God.

People thronged the streets, waiting for a glimpse of their pharaoh. The crowds parted for the soldiers escorting Seshta and her friends. People stared down from the rooftops, whispering about the dirty youngsters surrounded by guards.

They went to Miw's household, only a block from Pharaoh's local palace. Servants met them and led them to separate bathing chambers. They washed Seshta and dressed her in borrowed clothes and jewelry so quickly that she barely had time to worry about what lay ahead.

She joined Horus, Reya, and Miw. Servant girls brought wheat bread with vegetable paste, roast quail, almonds, and dates. Reya dug into the food as if he hadn't eaten in days. His bruises, some fresh and purple and some fading to yellow, stood out against his clean skin, but he smiled at Seshta.

Horus, in a crisp linen kilt and beaded broad collar that made him look like a noble, fidgeted and picked at the food. Seshta inhaled the spicy scents and her stomach growled. Her fatigue fled as she reached for a piece of steaming meat. Her heart swirled with questions, but she couldn't ask them with her mouth full.

When they finished, Miw said, "Let us go to the palace now."

Horus gulped. "I didn't do anything. I'll just go home and see Mother, she'll be worried, I've been gone all night—"

"I sent her a message," Miw said. "And Pharaoh is expecting you. I'm sure you don't want to disappoint him."

Horus's brown skin looked muddy and he hunched into his shoulders. "No," he whispered.

"It's all right." Seshta took Horus's hand in one of hers and Reya's in the other. "We'll be together."

Reya nodded. Clasping hands, they trailed after Miw.

The sun blazed in the sky by the time they reached the palace. They stood on the main steps amid a group of high officials to watch the procession approach.

Horus pressed close to Seshta and glanced anxiously at the richly dressed nobles around them. Seshta squeezed his hand. She had been to the palace a few times when Pharaoh wasn't there. Horus would never have dared to enter the gates. To a peasant like him, seeing Pharaoh from a distance might be the highlight of a lifetime. He would never imagine meeting the Son of Ra in person. No wonder he looked more frightened now than in the stable.

The roar of the crowd started in the distance. It grew, like the river in flood, as Pharaoh drew near. The entire city had come out to welcome the Living God.

The procession entered the palace gates. Sit-Hathor led the dancers. Behind her, the other girls swayed, spun, and tapped out intricate steps. The older priestesses shook sistrums and chanted, the music as bright and cheerful as laughter in the morning sun.

Seshta sighed as her rival did one of her famous backbends. "She looks wonderful. She doesn't even look tired, and they've come all the way from the docks."

Sit-Hathor's face shone with joy and pride as the dancers entered the palace. Seshta's lips trembled and she blinked moist eyes. It should have been her. If only she'd had the chance to compete!

She shook away the thought. Sit-Hathor might have won anyway. But even to be one of the dancers behind Sit-Hathor, just to dance for Pharaoh, the Living God, a memory to cherish when she grew old and stiff....

Horus grabbed her arm. "Look! It's one of those giraffes like I was trying to make."

Seshta gaped at the strange beast parading through the gate with its head as high as the pillars. "It does have a long neck! Amazing!"

"The world is full of strange things," Miw said. "Come, you will meet Pharaoh in the reception hall."

Seshta, Horus, and Reya gazed at each other with wide eyes. Meeting the Living God was a great honor, but suddenly the hearty breakfast sat like mud in Seshta's stomach. Would Pharaoh think her heroic for trying to save Reya, or a fool for walking into Meryey's trap? Would he know that she had never once thought of him, that in her worry about Reya she missed seeing the danger to Pharaoh?

The drums, chanting, and cheering of the procession faded behind them. They walked through a columned hall with murals on the walls and floor. Two massive Nubian guards stood in front of huge double doors covered in sheets of gold. Horus jerked back at the sight. Seshta gripped his hand, afraid he would run away.

"This way." Miw led them through a small door to one side. "We'll wait in here."

Horus's hand relaxed in Seshta's, but their palms were slick with nervous sweat. She wasn't sure how much of it was his and how much hers.

Several men stood clustered in the room, deep in conversation. They wore the dress of court officials: long, pleated kilts, formal wigs, and gold jewelry. Seshta barely glanced at the men until one broke away from the others and approached them.

"Is my father here yet?" Miw asked.

"No, little cat, he's with Pharaoh." The man's voice sounded familiar. Seshta studied him more closely. He grinned and winked at her. "Greetings... Idut."

"Ker?" she stammered. A wig hid his sidelock, and a blue-and-red broad collar draped his shoulders in place of the cowhide cloak.

The young Libu and Miw stepped away, talking softly together. Seshta, still gaping, turned to Horus, who shrugged.

"Who's that?" Reya whispered. "Why did he call you Idut?"

"He's... a friend, I guess," Seshta said. "I'll tell you about it later."

The slap of many feet hitting the floor in unison filled the hall outside. Dozens of guards passed by in formation. Among them Seshta caught a glimpse of men carrying a litter draped in rich cloth of many colors. On top sat the life-size golden statue of a god.

The god moved. Seshta realized that it wasn't a statue. It was Pharaoh.

Horus gasped and shrank back from the door.

"Relax," Reya snapped, although he didn't look or sound relaxed himself.

"But he's the Living God!" Horus gasped. "I can't go before him! I'm nobody. What if he speaks to me? What will I do?"

Seshta took hold of his shoulders and glared into his face. "You'll answer him. You deserve to be here."

She glanced at Reya and tried to sound confident. "We all do."

Chapter 25

Seshta kept her head bowed as they entered the throne room. No one could look Pharaoh in the face unless commanded to do so. From the top edge of her vision she could see the dais, with Pharaoh's feet resting between the lion-paw legs of his golden throne. Miw led them forward, dropped to her knees, and touched her forehead to the floor. Seshta did the same. Reya and Horus, of a lower status, flung themselves flat-out on their stomachs.

"You may rise." Pharaoh sounded like a god should, with a deep, slow, powerful voice. A shiver ran through Seshta as she got to her feet. She longed to look up into his face, to see clearly this man who was so much more than a man. She contented herself with gazing through lowered lashes at his brown feet in gilded sandals.

"Well, Miw, are you going to introduce your friends?"

Seshta's glance shot to Miw. The Living God had addressed her by name!

Miw smiled. She didn't look intimidated by the closeness of Pharaoh. "Ramses the Third, Lord of Upper and Lower Egypt, The Horus of Gold, Lord of the Sedge and the Bee, Son of Ra. May I present, first, one of your loyal soldiers, Reya, son of Bemenamun."

Reya bent to prostate himself again, but Pharaoh said, "Stay." Reya stood so tense that Seshta could see the veins bulging in his forearms.

"You are the young soldier," Pharaoh said, "who suspected a plot against me. You may speak."

"Yes, your majesty," Reya whispered.

"And you endured several days of captivity. I see you bear the marks."

Reya didn't speak for several moments. Then his voice came low and tense. "I was foolish. I trusted the wrong person. I humbly beg your forgiveness for my mistake, which could have caused so much misery. I only hope that the worthy General Kha'i will give me a chance to redeem myself."

Pharaoh chuckled. "General Kha'i was a bit put out when he heard of your accusations, weren't you, my friend?"

Someone grunted and Seshta glanced back to see the stocky, scarred form of General Kha'i pacing behind them. Beside her Reya hunched his shoulders as if waiting for a blow.

Pharaoh said, "I fear it is not your fate to be a foot soldier, Reya, son of Bemenamun."

Reya dropped to his knees. "Please, your majesty! I will make amends, I promise!"

"You misunderstand me," Pharaoh said. "I am not displeased. You've done well enough for a boy of your age. At least Miw's father seems to think so. The Eyes and Ears of Pharaoh has requested that you be relieved from your duties as a soldier so that he may train you himself."

Reya's head jerked up, but he forced it back down before his eyes could reach Pharaoh. Seshta glanced to the side and saw Miw's father standing with an arm over his daughter's shoulders. Miw winked at Seshta.

The Eyes and Ears of Pharaoh stepped in front of Reya. "Well, boy, what do you think? It won't be easy. I'll work you twice as hard as General Kha'i ever did."

"It would be a great honor," Reya said.

Miw's father held out his hand. Reya took it and rose, his face glowing.

Miw put an arm around Horus. "Next, oh Strong Bull Risen in Thebes, may I present Horus, son of Hor-mose, apprentice toymaker."

"Ah, yes, my youngest son loves your wooden hedgehog."

Horus's mouth opened and closed silently. Seshta remembered Ker examining the toy at the party. He must have kept it and passed it on to Pharaoh.

"I would like all the royal children to enjoy your gifts," Pharaoh said. "Therefore, you will join my royal workshop. You will work with the finest woods and even gold, silver, and precious stones if you wish."

Horus's mouth stayed open.

"Miw tells me you have a mother and a blind sister. I would not ask you to leave them. We will move them into more comfortable quarters near the palace."

Seshta could see the corner of Horus's smile in his flushed, down-turned face. He nodded quickly. Miw released him and he backed up.

Seshta's heart thudded painfully in her chest. She would be next.

Miw said, "And finally, oh Powerful Crowns, my sister at the Temple of Hathor, Seshta, daughter of Thanuro."

"The dancer who uncovered a spy." Pharaoh's voice held a smile. "I admire young women who carry the qualities of Neith, goddess of war, known for both love and courage. You have served me well."

Seshta's insides twisted with guilt. She glanced at Miw and licked her lips.

Miw raised her eyebrows. "You wish to speak?"

Seshta bobbed her head.

Pharaoh said, "Speak freely then."

"Your majesty," Seshta said, "I did not serve you at all. I did not realize this had anything to do with you until last night, when it was too late. I was searching for my friend Reya, that is all."

"Look at me."

Trembling, Seshta raised her head. She saw first the gold draping his body, which had made her think him a statue. Then she gazed into the face of Pharaoh. Fine lines etched his brown skin. He had a strong chin and large, kohl-lined eyes that looked solemn but kind.

"Every Egyptian is my child," he said, "and I am responsible for them all. By serving one of them, you serve me. If everyone acted with love and courage out of loyalty to their friends, I wouldn't need soldiers or guards, tax collectors or spies. You, too, have been my eyes."

Seshta gazed into Pharaoh's brown eyes. Her heartbeat slowed. Her muscles relaxed. She smiled.

"Your friends have received their rewards," he said. "What do you wish for yourself?"

Seshta hesitated. "I have my friends, alive and well. That is all I need."

Pharaoh chuckled. "Well said. But forget modesty. There must be something else that would please you. Name your gift."

Seshta glanced at Miw, who grinned and nodded. Seshta said in a rush, "To dance. That's all I've ever wanted. I was supposed to be in the contest, but—" She took a deep breath to stop her babbling. "I want to dance for you."

"Now?"

Seshta bowed her head and whispered, "If it pleases your majesty."

"So be it." Pharaoh clapped his hands. "Clear the floor," he called out. "Bring the musicians. We will have entertainment."

The room burst into activity. Laughing, Miw grabbed Seshta's arm and led her aside. She helped Seshta remove her jewelry, dress, and short court wig. Someone brought a wig with bells on the ends of a hundred long braids. They brought strings of rattling beads for her waist, wrists, and ankles. In moments, it seemed, she was dressed. She stood trembling and breathing fast, hands clenched into fists.

Reya kissed her cheek. "Good luck. You'll be wonderful, as always."

Horus nodded, smiling too hard to speak.

Miw said, "Have fun."

Seshta closed her eyes and breathed deeply. She shut out the world and thought only of the life force flowing through her body. She heard the musicians start playing as if from far away. She began to sway and tap her feet. Seshta raised her face and smiled.

And she danced.

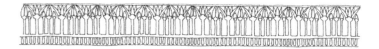

Author's Note

One of the earliest civilizations in the world arose in Egypt over 5000 years ago. The pharaohs ruled Egypt for 2500 years—but not without challenges.

Ramses the Third ruled during the New Kingdom, the golden age of Egypt. At that time, the great pyramids were already a thousand years old. Egypt remained the first and greatest superpower of the world, a land of plenty with rich fields fed by the annual Nile floods.

Foreigners flocked to Egypt as immigrants and traders, seeking a better life. But when Egypt closed its borders to foreigners facing famine at home, resentment sometimes turned to violence. In his 30 years as Pharaoh, from about 1184 to 1153 BC, Ramses had to defend the borders at least three times from foreign invaders. These included the Libu, a tribe from the area that is now Libya. His military also traveled to distant lands to meet foreign enemies.

At home, Ramses faced threats from the priesthood, a workers' strike at the royal necropolis, and even a palace murder plot.

The story of Seshta, Horus, and Reya is set during this time. Other than Ramses the Third, all characters and events are fictional, yet their lifestyles and attitudes are based on what we know of ancient Egypt.

The Eyes and Ears of Pharaoh was a real position at the head of Egypt's secret police. Young dancers performed at parties or worked in the temples. An ambitious young man might join the military, hoping for advancement. A poor boy might feel lucky to work as an apprentice toymaker.

Religion was part of everyday life, but individual devotion varied, and most people had a favorite god or goddess from among the large pantheon that watched over Egypt. (Seshta takes her name from the goddess of learning.) People believed the *ba*, part of the soul, traveled at night in dreams.

I have tried to reach across the millennia and capture life in ancient Egypt. Most of all, these characters were created with the belief that in every culture, throughout history, people are motivated by the same emotions; that no matter our age or background we can do great things if we work together; and that nothing is more precious than a good friend.

For more information about ancient Egypt, visit my website at www.chriseboch.com for a list of resources plus lesson plans to use in the classroom.

Chris Eboch

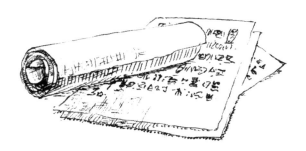

About the Author

Chris Eboch writes a variety of genres for all ages.

In *The Well of Sacrifice*, a Mayan girl in ninth-century Guatemala rebels against the High Priest who sacrifices anyone challenging his power.

Jesse Owens: Young Record Breaker and *Milton Hershey: Young Chocolatier* are inspirational biographies in Simon & Schuster's Childhood of Famous Americans series, written under the name M.M. Eboch.

The Haunted series for ages 8-12 follows a brother and sister who travel with their parents' ghost hunter TV show. They try to help the ghosts, while keeping their activities secret from meddling grownups. In *The Ghost on the Stairs*, an 1880s ghost bride haunts a Colorado hotel, waiting for her missing husband to return. *The Riverboat Phantom* features a steamboat pilot still trying to prevent a long-ago disaster. In *The Knight in the Shadows*, a Renaissance French squire protects a sword on display at a New York City museum. During *The Ghost Miner's Treasure*, Jon and Tania help a dead man find his lost gold mine—but they're not the only ones looking for it.

Read excerpts at www.chriseboch.com.

Ms. Eboch also writes novels for adults under the name Kris Bock. Learn more at www.krisbock.com.

About the Art:

Cover artist Lois Bradley has been a working New Mexico artist since 1992. She has been involved with the design, illustration, and production on several book projects, most recently as the illustrator for Blind Tom: The Horse Who Helped Build the Great Railroad, by Shirley Raye Redmond (Mountain Press Publishing), a New Mexico Book Award finalist. The award-wining artist is currently represented by Framing Concepts Gallery in Albuquerque, New Mexico. See her work at www.loisbradley.com.

Rollin Thomas is an award-winning illustrator, author, designer, and educator. Whimsy and wit are his hallmarks. He likes making one-of-a-kind art books and limited editions of tiny hand-stitched books. Rollin teaches writing, arts, and illustration at all levels with enthusiasm. He has written 42 produced plays for children and is a contract artist-in-residence at Concord International Elementary School. As an area EMMY award-winning theatrical designer, Rollin has designed sets, masks, puppets, and costumes for over 230 plays, musicals, films, and operas.

Made in the USA
San Bernardino, CA
27 July 2016